"Dad!" Diego cried. "Lauren and Ryan and Maya and Poppy got a dog!"

"It's a hound-pointer mix, like, *this* big." Sofia held her hands a yardstick apart. "Come out and see!"

All three of Fiona's older kids, plus Eduardo's two, ran after the dog, leaving Fiona, Eduardo and Poppy to watch.

Eduardo blew out a sigh and tried not to notice the way the sun set fire to Fiona's hair. Or the curve of her smile as she watched her kids play. Or the unconsciously warm and motherly way she made little sounds in her throat to soothe her youngest, who still rested her head on Fiona's shoulder.

He didn't want to notice what a deep-down good person Fiona was. But being around her during all his at-home moments made that reality impossible to ignore.

Maybe he needed to start looking for a new place to live. Before he did something crazy again, like tell her how much he liked being around her.

Lee Tobin McClain read *Gone with the Wind* in the third grade and has been a hopeless romantic ever since. When she's not writing angst-filled love stories with happy endings, she's getting inspiration from her church singles group, her gymnastics-obsessed teenage daughter, and her rescue dog and cat. In her day job, Lee gets to encourage aspiring romance writers in Seton Hill University's low-residency MFA program. Visit her at leetobinmcclain.com.

Books by Lee Tobin McClain

Love Inspired

Rescue River

Engaged to the Single Mom
His Secret Child
Small-Town Nanny
The Soldier and the Single Mom
The Soldier's Secret Child
A Family for Easter

Christmas Twins

Secret Christmas Twins

Lone Star Cowboy League: Boys Ranch

The Nanny's Texas Christmas

A Family
for Easter

Lee Tobin McClain

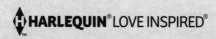

HARLEQUIN® LOVE INSPIRED®

Recycling programs
for this product may
not exist in your area.

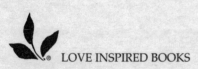

LOVE INSPIRED BOOKS

ISBN-13: 978-1-335-42794-6

A Family for Easter

Printed in U.S.A.

For God so loved the world, that he gave his only begotten Son, that whosoever believeth in him should not perish, but have everlasting life.
—*John* 3:16

To my dad, because we always visited his family at Easter, and because I know he's singing in the heavenly choir.

Chapter One

Fiona Farmingham clutched the edge of Chez La Ferme's elegant tablecloth and wished she were home on the couch with her kids, eating popcorn and watching movies. Wearing sweats and slippers rather than heels and a dress and shapewear.

Based on tonight, at least, dating was way overrated.

"You should come see me in Cleveland," Henry said loudly, forking braised lamb shank into his mouth. "We have restaurants that would put this place to shame. *Really* fancy."

She forced her face into something resembling a smile and pushed her roasted vegetables around her plate, not daring to look around at all the Rescue River customers and waitstaff Henry had probably just offended.

A throat cleared a couple of tables away, and

she glanced up. A soccer-dad friend, Eduardo Delgado, was looking over his date's shoulder, smiling at Fiona with what looked like sympathy.

Her tight shoulders relaxed a little. Eduardo's warm, friendly face reminded her of school parent nights and carpools and kids' league games. Her normal life.

She was a little surprised to see Eduardo, a single parent who worked as a groundsman at Hinton Enterprises, dining at their small Ohio town's only upscale restaurant. He never even bought himself nachos or a hot dog at the school concession stand, always relying on a cooler from home for himself and his two kids instead. She'd thought that meant he was economizing, but maybe he was just into eating healthy.

"Did you hear me?" Henry scooted his chair closer. "I have a nice big house. Six bedrooms and three-and-a-half bathrooms. You should come visit!"

Like *that* was going to happen. She channeled her society-perfect mother, who could out-polite the Queen of England, even managing a small smile. "With my kids, it's hard for me to get away."

"Yeah, four kids, that's a lot!" Henry shook his head and attacked his spring pea risotto with vigor. She turned her chair half away and pretended to hear a sound from the evening bag she hadn't used since attending society events with her late husband three years ago. She pulled out her cell phone and studied its blank screen. "Henry, I'm so sorry, but I think my kids need me." Not a lie; kids always needed their parents, hers in particular. Right now, though, it was *she* who needed her kids.

"I thought you said you had a sitter. I was hoping we could spend more time together."

"Thanks, but no, thanks. I really do have to go." Fiona tried to keep her voice low, even though half the restaurant's patrons had surely heard their discussion.

Why, oh, why had she let her friends Daisy and Susan talk her into online dating? But they'd both approved Henry's profile, and he'd sounded nice on the phone.

She knew why: because she thought her kids might benefit from having a man in their lives. And, maybe a tiny bit, because she wished for a male companion who would care for her, even love her, just as she was.

Fat chance of that, *fat* being the operative word.

"Look, Fiona." He gulped his drink and wiped a napkin across his mouth. "I wouldn't have sprung for this expensive dinner if I'd known…"

Fiona stood and grabbed her purse, thankful

she'd driven there in her own car. "Henry, it's been...*interesting* to meet you."

"Hey! You can't just leave in the middle of—"

"Actually, I can." She fumbled for her wallet. Why had she thought, for one minute, that she should try a relationship again?

"Can I help you?" Their waitress, a college-aged girl Fiona knew slightly, touched her forearm. Her curious expression made Fiona's stomach twist.

She swallowed and lifted her chin, her mother's training once again coming to her aid. "Thanks, yes, Mia. Separate checks, please, and I'm sure this will cover mine." She extracted two twenties and handed them to the waitress. Then she turned, keeping her eyes on the front door. If she didn't look to the right or the left, she could avoid the pitying stares that were surely coming her way.

"Oh, Mrs. Farmingham," Mia called after her, "that's way too much. You just had an appetizer and salad, and you didn't even order a drink!"

Let the world know I'm dieting, would you? "It's fine, keep the change."

"Just hang on a minute." It sounded like Henry's mouth was full. "How much was it?"

Father God, please just let me get home, and I'll forget about dating and just be happy being a mom. I'll delete my online profile. I'll avoid the matchmakers at the Senior Towers. She hurried away from the sound of Henry's bargaining with poor Mia, toward freedom.

Outside, the spring breeze cooled her cheeks. With just an hour of daylight left, the setting sun was nestled in the clouds, turning the sky pink and gold.

She took deep breaths of the rich, fragrant farm-town air and reminded herself that she'd been through far worse than a bad date and had survived.

Behind her, she heard the restaurant door opening and the sound of voices, including Henry's calling for her to wait.

She quickened her pace and stumbled a little. *Slow down. This is embarrassing enough without you falling on your face.* She reached her SUV, and the sight of her kids' car seats, the snack bags scattered across the floor, reminded her once again of her priorities.

Her kids were what was important. Not a man. Men ridiculed and cheated on women like her.

She was opening the door when Henry caught up with her. "Hey, come on, what did I say wrong?" He grabbed her arm. "I like big gals!"

Seriously bad pickup line, buddy. She jerked away and started to climb into the driver's seat. Not as easy in a dress and heels as in her usual mom uniform of jeans and sneakers, but she managed.

He didn't let go of her forearm, and his finger-tips pushed deeper into her skin. "What are you waiting for?" he asked, leaning in, standing on tiptoe. "You're not getting any younger, and in a cow town like this, you're never going to meet anyone— Hey!" Suddenly, his hand was off her. There was a low rough exchange of words, and then Henry was gone.

In his place stood Eduardo Delgado, the sun-set glowing golden behind him. "Everything okay, Fiona? I got worried when he followed you out."

She let her head rest on the steering wheel for just a few seconds. "Thank you. I… He didn't want to leave me alone."

"He will now." A smile tweaked up the cor-ners of Eduardo's mouth as he gestured toward Henry, sliding into a silver Jaguar and slamming the door behind himself. The car started with a powerful roar and then backed out too fast, tires squealing. A moment later, Henry was gone.

"Wow. What did you say to him?"

"I explained how we treat women here in Res-cue River. He decided he didn't fit in."

A surprised chuckle escaped her. Eduardo without his kids was…different.

She wondered if he'd heard that comment

about *big gals*. She hoped not. Not because she especially cared what Eduardo thought. It was just…mortifying. "Thanks for taking time out of your date to rescue me."

"It's no problem. My date was a bust, too." His mouth twisted a little to one side as he leaned back against her open car door. He was a big man, his muscles visible even in his suit jacket. Which made sense, given the kind of work he did.

"Where *is* your date?" she asked, looking around the parking lot.

"She left. Bad match."

Fiona lifted an eyebrow. "Don't tell me you're online dating, too."

"No. No way. But I did some work at the Senior Towers, and…" He looked down at the ground, shaking his head as a grin tugged at the side of his mouth.

"You let the ladies get to you!" Fiona laughed outright. "Nonna D'Angelo, right? She's relentless."

"They triple-teamed me. Nonna and Miss Minnie and Lou Ann Miller. Apparently, their matchmaking business is taking off, and they needed more men to participate."

"And you started at Chez La Ferme?"

"That's how they do it. They worked with the restaurant to cut first-time couples a special deal." He was studying her curiously. "How well did you know your date?"

"Not at all. This was our first meeting." She wrinkled her nose. "And our last."

They smiled at each other, that eye-rolling sympathetic smile of fellow sufferers.

Eduardo's phone pinged, and he pulled it out of his pocket and studied the face of it. Then he spun away and raced toward the other side of the parking lot.

"What's wrong?" She climbed out of the SUV.

"Fire at my place!" he called over his shoulder.

"Oh, no! What can I do to help?" She ran a few steps toward him, then stopped. If he needed her, she should take her own car.

"Sitter says kids are okay!" he called as he climbed into a truck with the logo *Delgado Landscaping* on the side.

An unrelated thought—*I didn't know he ran his own landscaping business in addition to working for Hinton Enterprises*—distracted her. Par for the course. "Fiona brain," her brother had called it. She shook her head, refocused in time to see Eduardo pulling out of the parking lot, his phone to his ear.

Fiona started her car and pulled out. She'd run home and check on the kids, get them into bed and see if the sitter could stay late. Then she'd go check on Eduardo. Even though he'd said his kids were fine, a fire could be devastating. They might need some help she could offer.

Eduardo slammed on the brakes in front of his rented duplex. No flames, but there were flashing lights, caustic smoke and men's voices registered as he looked around, fixated on just one thing: finding his kids.

"Papa!" Sofia called.

Eduardo turned toward the voice. When he saw Sofia and Diego running toward him, he knelt, opened his arms and clutched them to him, his throat tight.

His children had been at risk. He could have lost them.

Through his own negligence, just like with their mother. He had no plans to get involved with someone else, so why had he left his children with a sitter so he could go on a silly date?

He felt a hand on his shoulder. "They've had a scare, but they were never in danger," said Lou Ann Miller, his babysitter. In her late seventies, she was sharper and more agile than a lot of people half her age.

Her words calmed him and he stood, keeping a hand on each child's shoulder. "You're all right, Lou Ann? What happened?"

"We're all fine, and the fire seems to be contained to the bathroom," she said. "But no thanks to a smoke alarm, and you really ought to talk to your landlord about that."

"*I* was the one who smelled the smoke," Diego announced.

"And I ran out in the hall and saw fire!" Sofia leaned close to Eduardo. "It was scary, Papa. Miss Lou Ann made us run across the street to the Silvases' house and call 911."

"And she broke the door of the new neighbors to get them out!" Diego's voice sounded impressed. "She used a hammer!"

Eduardo's heartbeat was returning to normal, and he looked up at Lou Ann.

"They weren't answering the door, and since it's a duplex…" She shrugged apologetically. "I broke a window and reached in to unlock their door. They'd fallen asleep and didn't hear the doorbell or the knocking."

He looked at her quizzically. "They were sleeping heavily this early in the evening?"

"Very," she said, meeting his eyes with meaning in her own. "Pretty much passed out."

From what Eduardo had seen of the new neighbors, drinking or drugs had probably been involved. "They're okay?"

She nodded. "The fire turned out to be small and the firefighters contained it quickly. They interviewed me and the kids already, but they'll probably want to talk to you as well."

"Of course." As he made arrangements for Lou Ann to take the kids to her house and gave them more hugs and praise, his mind chewed on one pressing problem.

He *had* to get his kids into a safer home.

He'd chosen this place because it was inexpensive, in a decent neighborhood with a good-sized yard. When would he learn that his instincts were terrible when it came to keeping his family safe? Hadn't Elizabeth's death proved that?

A busy hour later, Eduardo sat on a concrete wall outside his wet, smoking home. They were fortunate that it was unseasonably warm for mid-March. As he watched firefighters and a police inspector finish examining the smoke and water damage, he tried to think about what to do next.

The firefighters had kept the flames from spreading to the shared attic, limiting the damage to just the Delgados' bathroom. Apparently, when the men had pulled the ceiling down, they'd found insulation smoldering around an exhaust fan.

Eduardo clenched his fists, then consciously took a couple of deep breaths. The most important thing was that no one had been injured.

Police Chief Dion Coleman, who lived the next street over and seemed to know everything happening in the town, sat down beside him. "You okay, man?"

"Not really." Eduardo looked blankly as neighbors gathered near the fire truck in the deepening twilight. On the other side of the yard, their landlord was still talking to an inspector, gesticulating wildly.

"I spoke with one of the firefighters, and he says damage looks minimal. You could probably move back in within a couple of weeks, and insurance would pay—"

"No." Even the thought of taking his kids back inside the duplex appalled Eduardo. "We'll be looking for somewhere else to live. Somewhere safe."

"I understand." Dion leaned forward, elbows on his knees, weaving his fingers together. "Rental market around here is tight, though. Where are your kids now?"

"Lou Ann Miller took them in for the night." Eduardo gestured down the street toward the older woman's house. "She was babysitting when it happened. I'm going to crash on her couch later, too, if I can even sleep."

"This kind of thing can prey on your mind," Dion said. "But you know the good Lord's got you in His hand, right? Your kids, too."

"Right." Eduardo didn't want to go into his fear that if Lou Ann and the kids hadn't been awake and alert, the Lord might not have seen fit to save them. Not to mention the fact that the

Lord *hadn't* had Elizabeth in His hands when she'd struggled with cancer.

Or maybe it was just Eduardo himself who excelled at letting his family down.

Dion stood. "If you need anything, you know where to find me." And he was gone.

Eduardo rubbed a hand across his face, and all of a sudden, Fiona Farmingham was in the spot Dion had vacated beside Eduardo on the concrete wall. "Eduardo, is there anything I can do to help?"

He squinted at her pretty features framed by long wavy red hair. "What are you doing here?"

"I was worried. After I got my kids settled, I came over to see if there was anything I could do."

"You have a sitter?" he asked inanely. He was still trying to process everything that had happened tonight. His brain seemed to be running at reduced speed.

"Yes, and I talked to her. She's fine with staying later, and she put the kids to bed. But you have bigger things on your mind. Is there anything you and the kids need?"

He lifted his hands, palms up. "No. I'm just trying to figure out what to do. I have to find a new place to live."

"It's a total loss?"

"No, not much damage. But this happened

because of an electrical issue." He slammed his fist into his hand, shaking his head. "I *knew* there were maintenance problems, that the landlord wasn't keeping the place up. I should have moved us out months ago."

Hesitantly, she put a hand on his arm. "That must make you really mad. But the kids are okay. And you're okay." She squeezed his arm lightly and then pulled her hand back. "You can figure out who's to blame later, even think about legal action. For now, you need to decide about the day-to-day stuff, what to do."

Her voice was husky, calm, soothing. A little of the tension left his shoulders, chased away by the strange feeling that he had someone at his side, shoulder to shoulder. "Yeah. That's right."

She nodded briskly. "Your kids are settled for the night? And you have a place to sleep?"

"Lou Ann Miller's house," he said, nodding.

"Do you need clothes, toiletries, pajamas?"

"I don't think so. I think they're going to let me back in pretty soon, take me around and let me gather up some stuff. There'll be an investigation, but it's pretty clear the problem started with some faulty wiring in the bathroom exhaust fan. The smoke alarm malfunctioned, too, apparently." He shook his head. "I've got to find a new place to live."

She looked thoughtful for a moment, and then

she nodded as if she'd made a decision. "You could stay in my carriage house."

"What?" He cocked his head at her and frowned.

"It's a complete three-bedroom little home. Used to be where people kept their carriages, and then it was a spare garage, but the previous owners modified it into a space that could work as an office or a rental. I was using it for... Doesn't matter." She waved her hand. "I've been planning to advertise for a tenant, anyway."

Eduardo looked at Fiona. Her eyes held concern and the desire to help. The woman was kind and good, but he didn't feel comfortable with the spur-of-the-moment offer. "I don't see... We probably can't make that work," he said. "You have your own plans for the place. And anyway, I'm looking for something really safe, up to code, after what happened here."

She glared at him. "Do you think I'd offer you a place that was dangerous or unsound?"

Oh, man, now he'd upset this kind woman who was only trying to help. "Of course not. I'm sorry. I'm a mess."

"Understandable." She stood up, something like insecurity creeping into her eyes. "I'm sure you have other options, but if you want to talk more about the place, I'll be at church tomorrow."

She bent down, put her arms around his shoulders for an awkward hug and then disappeared into the darkness.

Exhausted as he was by the events of the evening, Eduardo was awake enough to feel a particular warmth where she'd touched him.

Chapter Two

The next day, Fiona and her four kids walked—or in Ryan's and Maya's case, ran—out of the little white clapboard church on the edge of Rescue River.

"Careful!" Fiona called. "Stay on the sidewalk!" But she couldn't help smiling at her middle two children's joy. Maya's exuberance didn't surprise her—at seven, Maya was her wild child—but Ryan, though only two years older, tended to be way too serious. It was good to see him run and play.

Beside Fiona, ten-year-old Lauren walked with more decorum, as befitted the dignity of the eldest child. Little Poppy nudged in between Fiona and Lauren and then reached up to grab their hands. "Swing me," she ordered with the confidence of a three-year-old, and Fiona and

Lauren held her hands tight while she jumped up, swinging her legs.

"Hey," Ryan called back to them, "there's Diego and Sofia!"

Fiona's heart gave a tiny little leap as she looked ahead and saw Eduardo and his two kids walking in the same direction Fiona was heading. She always parked near the church's little play area, and today Eduardo's truck was next to her SUV.

Had he decided to take her up on her offer of the carriage house?

She'd seen Eduardo dressed up once before, on his date at Chez La Ferme, but he looked happier and more comfortable today, in his dark suit and open-collared blue shirt, laughing with his kids.

"Sofia! Hey!" Lauren dropped Poppy's hand and ran toward the Delgados. Ryan followed suit. They played on the same coed soccer team with Sofia and Diego, and the four children were becoming friends.

A moment later, all of them were on the grass next to their vehicles. Ryan, Diego and Maya darted back and forth, burning off energy by throwing around the cotton-ball lambs they'd made in Sunday school.

"Is that sacrilegious, to play with the Easter lamb?" Fiona asked, half-joking.

"Is it, Dad?" Diego clutched his lamb to his chest, his expression anxious.

Eduardo looked amused. "Not really. In some cultures, kids raise a lamb for Easter. I'm sure they play with it."

"That would be fun!" Maya danced over to Fiona. "Can we get a lamb, Mom?"

"No." Fiona tried to tuck Maya's hair back into its ponytail holder without much success. "But we're thinking about a dog when summer comes, and you kids can all help pick it out."

"Yes!" Maya pumped her arm in the air and ran back to the game of toss-the-lamb.

Fiona glanced over at Eduardo. "I don't think the kids would like what happens to the pet lamb at Easter."

"Easter dinner?" He winced. "Good point."

"Mom, can me and Sofia swing Poppy?" Lauren asked.

Poppy threw her arms around Lauren. "Please, Mommy? I wanna swing with LaLa!"

"If you're careful. Not too high."

"I *know*, Mom. Come on, Sofia." Lauren picked Poppy up easily and carried her toward the swing set. At ten, she was tall and broad-shouldered, often mistaken for a teenager.

"Poppy's cute," Eduardo said, looking a little wistful. "I remember those days."

"They go by too fast." Fiona didn't want to

think about how she wasn't going to get another baby, how Poppy was her last. So, she watched as Lauren set her little sister on a swing, giving her a stern lecture about holding on tight. Lauren liked to show off her childcare skills, and Sofia was a new audience.

Which was fine. To a pair of ten-year-olds, a toddler seemed like a doll, and Poppy was glad to play that role if it got her some big-girl attention.

Fiona and Eduardo stood together, watching their happy kids. Was the question of the carriage house hanging between them, making things awkward, or was it just her being silly?

She focused her attention on a robin pecking at the newly turned earth, pulling out a fat earthworm.

It was a beautiful spring day and the service had been uplifting, and there was no need to feel uncomfortable with family friends. If he didn't want to take her up on her offer, that was perfectly fine. He probably had lots of friends to reach out to.

"If you were serious about renting to us," Eduardo said to Fiona, "could we stop over and check out the carriage house sometime soon? I've been online and in the paper, and there's not much out there to rent. I have an appointment to look at a trailer out on County Line Road, but it's a little more isolated than I'm comfortable with."

"Sure!" Fiona heard the enthusiasm in her own voice and toned it down. "Come out this afternoon, if you'd like. And you know, I also have a landscaping project I need done. Maybe you could take a look."

"Are they coming over?" Maya had overheard, and a big smile broke out on her face.

"Maybe," Fiona said.

"They might come over!" Maya rushed over to the big girls with her important news, followed by Diego and Ryan.

"They're obviously on board," Fiona said. "In fact, you're welcome to come for some lunch. I have plenty of hot dogs and burgers—"

"No, thank you," Eduardo interrupted, a shadow crossing his face. "That's a nice invitation, but we have other plans."

Heat rose in Fiona's face, and she was sure it showed in her cheeks. The disadvantage of being a fair-skinned redhead.

The rebuff was so definite. He didn't want to come. "I just thought… It's always hard to figure out what to do for lunch after church, at least it is for me, and so if you needed…" *Stop talking. He doesn't want to be your friend.*

"As far as helping with your landscaping…" He trailed off.

"It was just an idea. I know you have a lot going on."

He looked at the ground and then met her eyes with a forthright gaze. "You didn't suggest it to be charitable?"

"*Charitable?* What you do mean?"

"I just thought… Since we're going to struggle a little, given what's happened, maybe you were trying to help. And that's not necessary." His chin lifted.

"I'm sorry to say that didn't even occur to me," she admitted. "I've been meaning to look for a landscaper, but I haven't gotten around to it. When I saw from your truck that you do landscaping, it seemed providential. If you're not interested, it's no problem."

He opened his mouth to answer. But the kids had been conferring over by the swings, and before he could say anything, they ran over in a group.

"Are Sofia and Diego coming over?" Ryan was obviously the designated speaker.

Fiona glanced up at Eduardo, eyebrow lifted. His call.

"Yes, I think so," he said. "A little later."

"Well, we were wondering…" Ryan glanced at his big sister.

"We figured out a plan." A winning smile

broke across Lauren's face. "Can Sofia ride with us?"

"And can I ride with Diego?" Ryan asked. "Please, Mom? I like their truck."

"That won't work." Fiona looked over at Eduardo. "They're coming over later in the afternoon. Right?"

"We have a stop to make," Eduardo said, putting a hand on Diego's shoulder and another on Sofia's.

"Oh, yeah. I forgot," Sofia said. "We're going to the cemetery."

"How come?" Ryan asked.

"Our mom is there," Diego explained.

"Well, her grave is," Sofia clarified. "Mama's in heaven."

"I *know* she's in heaven. I'm not a dummy." Diego's face reddened, and he opened his mouth as if to say more. But Eduardo squeezed his shoulder and, when Diego looked up, shook his head.

Diego's shoulders slumped.

"Our dad's in heaven, too." Ryan bumped against Diego's arm in a friendly way and then dug up a pebble with his toe, booting it down the sidewalk. That was Ryan, kindhearted and empathetic. "C'mon!"

Diego pulled away from his father and jogged alongside Ryan, kicking a stone of his own.

"If she's in heaven," Maya said, looking up at Sofia and Eduardo, "then why are you going to the cemetery?"

Fiona blew out a breath and squatted down beside her inquisitive seven-year-old. "Every family does things differently. A lot of people like to put flowers on a loved one's grave."

"I'll show you," Sofia said, tugging the truck key out of her father's hand. She clicked open the vehicle and pulled a pot of hyacinths from the passenger side. "Today, we're gonna put these on Mama's grave."

"They're pretty." Maya stood on tiptoe to sniff the fragrant blossoms. "I never saw a cemetery."

Fiona didn't correct her. Of course, Maya had been at her father's funeral, together with the other kids, including Poppy, who'd been just two months old.

"Some of the graves have tricycles on them, or teddy bears," Sofia announced. "That's kids who died."

"Sofia." Eduardo gestured toward Poppy, obviously urging silence in front of a little one.

"Sorry," Sofia whispered and then squatted down on her haunches, holding out the flowers to Poppy. "Want to smell?"

Poppy did and then giggled as the flowers tickled her nose. Distraction accomplished.

"Can we go with them?" Lauren asked unexpectedly.

Fiona opened her mouth and then closed it again. She knew it was important to deal with kids' questions about death, but really? "We don't want to intrude," she said, putting a hand on Lauren's shoulder. "It's their private family time."

"We don't care," Diego said as he passed by, chasing the rock he was kicking. "We go all the time."

They *did*? Fiona couldn't help glancing at Eduardo curiously. He must still be grieving hard for his wife.

"We go once every month," Sofia corrected her little brother.

"Why don't we go to our daddy's grave, Mom?" Maya asked.

"Because our daddy was bad," Lauren said before Fiona could put together a response.

Poppy tugged at Fiona's hand. "Was our daddy bad?"

Pain and concern twisted Fiona's stomach, along with anger at Reggie. He'd hurt her, badly, but even worse was how he'd hurt his children.

Nonetheless, she knew what she had to do: keep her own feelings inside and be positive about the children's father, lest they grow up worrying that they themselves carried something bad inside them. "He was your daddy who loved you and there was lots that was good about him," she said, making sure her voice was loud enough for all the kids to hear. "But his grave is back in Illinois, where we used to live."

"Our mom was the best," Diego said. "Daddy has a picture." He tugged the keys out of his sister's hands and showed the photo attached to the ring.

Fiona squinted down at it, and Lauren and Maya leaned in to see as well. A petite dark-haired woman held a baby, with a little girl who must be Sofia leaning into her. Eduardo stood behind the woman, arms protectively around his whole family.

"She's really pretty," Maya said.

"*Was* pretty," Lauren corrected in her automatic big-sister mode, then reddened and looked over at Sofia. "I'm sorry your mom died."

Sofia nodded and leaned back against her father, who knelt and put an arm around her. Taking back the key ring from Diego, he held it so Sofia could see. "She was very pretty. Just a tiny little thing, but strong. You look a lot like her."

"I don't," Diego said, obviously parroting what he'd heard before. "I look more like you."

"Your mother loved both of you very much."

Eduardo squeezed Sofia's shoulders, let her go and then patted Diego on the back. "She loved to cook for you, and play with you, and read to you. We'll talk about her at the cemetery, like we always do."

Fiona's throat tightened. Helping kids through the loss of a parent was an ongoing challenge.

"Do we have a picture of our daddy?" Maya asked. "Because…" She looked up at Fiona, her face uncertain. "I don't really remember what he looks like."

"Back home in our albums, stupid," Lauren said.

"We don't call each other stupid," Fiona said automatically. "And, speaking of back home, we should get going and leave the Delgados to do what they were planning to do." Maya still looked unhappy—rare for her—so Fiona stooped down and grasped her hands. "Do you want to look at our albums when we go home? There are some good pictures of you and Daddy."

"Okay." Maya nodded, her momentary distress gone.

"Are we still having hot dogs?" Ryan asked. "I'm starving!"

"Yes. Come on, everyone in the car." Fiona clicked open the door locks and then looked at Eduardo. "I'm sorry for your loss."

He nodded, his eyes unreadable. "And I'm sorry for yours as well."

As Fiona drove home, her mind kept going back to Eduardo's family picture. Obviously, he wasn't over his tiny, beautiful, loving wife.

She had no right to feel jealous just because *she'd* struck out in the marriage game. It was nothing more than what her mother had always predicted—at her size, and not being the brightest woman around, attracting any man at all had been unlikely. The chances of him being a good, responsible, trustworthy person? Just about nil.

She had more than she deserved in her four wonderful children, and she was content with her life now, as it was.

Later that Sunday afternoon, Eduardo pulled up in front of Fiona's house, stopped the truck and waited. He knew exactly what his kids were going to say.

"*That's* their house?" Sofia asked. "It looks like it's from a movie!"

"It's cool," Diego said. "Is that where we'd live?"

"No. Mrs. Farmingham is looking to rent the carriage house, out back. I haven't seen it, but I'm sure it's nothing fancy."

Diego shrugged, then poked his sister in the side. "C'mon, let's go! There's Ryan!"

"Wait." Eduardo turned in his seat to face both of his kids. "We need to remember some things."

"I know. Good manners." Diego had his hand on the door handle.

"Like what?" he prompted.

"Wipe your feet, and say please and thank you, and be quiet inside the house." Sofia recited the list with an eye roll that previewed the teen she would soon become.

"Good." From the glove box, Eduardo pulled out two bags of *mazapán*, a round and chewy Mexican candy one of his aunts always sent them in quantity. He handed a bag to each child. "These are to share with everyone after we check with Mrs. Farmingham. She and I are going to be talking about work before we check out the carriage house, so I need you to be self-reliant. You can interrupt us if it's an emergency."

"Like fire or blood," Diego said, and Eduardo let out a short laugh. He should never have said that to the kids, but one night when he'd been working on the books for his landscaping business, he'd ordered his whining kids to watch TV and only disturb him under those circumstances.

Of course, that's what they remembered. "Right," he said, "or anything else that you think is important. You both have good judgment."

"Can we go now?" Sofia asked, and Eduardo looked at the house and saw that Fiona had come out onto the porch, holding Poppy on her hip. The other three kids were already on the stairs.

"Go ahead," he said, taking his time about gathering up his tablet and a couple of plant catalogs.

He climbed out slowly. Fiona stood listening to his kids, and he saw her smile and nod. Sofia and Diego distributed pieces of candy all around and gave the rest of the bags to Fiona; then all of the kids took off for the big side yard.

Fiona was wearing jeans and a puffy kind of blouse, light green, that made her red hair glow. Behind her, the old two-story Victorian mansion rose in splendor.

It was exactly the kind of house he'd have bought himself if he'd had the money. The yellow paint with green trim was nice, but best of all were the wraparound porches, one on the first floor and one on the second. A couple of red-brick chimneys indicated fireplaces inside and a turret at the top, with windows all around, would make a great playroom for kids.

Or a relaxing spot for parents to kick back and watch the sunset.

He straightened his shoulders and glanced down at his *Delgado Landscaping* shirt. He'd debated wearing just ordinary casual clothes, but that would have misrepresented the relationship.

He was aiming to rent a place from her and

maybe to do some work for her, too. She was a potential client and landlord, not a friend.

He walked briskly up the sidewalk and held out a hand to shake hers. "Hey, Fiona. Thanks for letting us see the carriage house. And for considering me for a landscaping job, too."

She lifted an eyebrow and shook his hand. "Of course."

Heat rose in the back of his neck. Why did he feel so awkward with her?

And her hand—which, he noticed, he was still grasping in his, and he let it go like a hot potato—wasn't the well-manicured, callus-free one he'd expected, but strong, with plain short-cut nails.

Long delicate fingers, too.

"So," he began.

"Would you like something—" she started at the same time.

They both laughed awkwardly. "Ladies first," he said and then wondered if that had sounded stupid.

"Um, okay." Her cheeks went pink. "What was I... Oh, yeah. Would you like something to drink? Coffee, soda, iced tea?"

"No, I'm fine. Thanks. And thanks for letting the kids come along. It's a big help."

"Sure. They're all having fun." She gestured across the yard.

The kids were running toward a play set situated near a tidy little outbuilding that must be the carriage house. Poppy couldn't keep up and called out to the others. Sofia turned, went back to the little girl and picked her up.

His heart did a funny little twist at the sight of his daughter holding a toddler. Sofia would *love* to have a little sister. He and Elizabeth had hoped for that, planned for it.

Plans don't always work out. "Does somebody live in your carriage house now?" he asked to distract himself.

"No. I was using it for my dog-walking business, but now..." She shrugged, looking away. "I just want to rent it out."

"You're not thinking of trying another business?"

"Well... I'd like to. But...no. Not for now." She crossed her arms over her chest.

Clear enough. None of my business. "Why don't you show me what you're thinking of doing in the yard first, since that'll take more time. I can look at the carriage house after."

"Okay, sure." She wiped her hands down the sides of her jeans. As she headed to the side yard, he fell into step beside her. It was nice that she was so tall. Easy for them to walk in step.

Unbidden, a memory of Elizabeth, scolding him for his tendency to outpace her, came to mind.

Fiona was talking, and he forced himself to focus. "So over here," she said, "I'm thinking about digging up this whole section and planting vegetables. Corn and tomatoes and squash and peppers. I'd like to maybe slope it south? To catch the sun?"

"That makes sense." He looked around the yard, measured it in his mind, pictured some ways it could look. "You thinking about raised beds?"

"Yes, if it's possible."

He nodded. "I think we could put in three small terraces. It would look good." He bent down, pinched up some soil and squeezed it between his thumb and forefinger. Thick and hard; too much clay. "You're going to need some soil amendments. In future years you can compost, if you're into that, but you'll probably have to shell out for commercial stuff this year. Peat moss, humus, maybe some mushroom compost. It'll cost you."

"That's not a problem," she said, and then a blush rose up her cheeks again and she looked away. "I…inherited some money. Nothing I earned myself."

He'd known she was wealthy. A lot of his customers were. As a professional, he could look at it as a good thing. "Hey, it's great you can afford to do that. It'll get your garden off to a strong start. Mind if I take some measurements?"

"That would be great. And here's the key to the carriage house. Go ahead and look around when you're done."

She checked on the kids while he measured and sketched. By the time they'd gotten around to the other side of the yard and discussed fruit trees and blueberry bushes, they were more at ease with each other. And when the kids came running up, thirsty, he helped her get drinks for everyone and accepted one himself.

While Fiona bandaged Ryan's scraped knee and helped Poppy change into a clean outfit—some kind of a mud puddle accident—Eduardo went out onto the porch and tried to get started on an estimate.

He found himself thinking about Fiona instead.

Specifically, about her past.

It was common knowledge in town that Fiona had been married to a wealthy man. And that her husband had turned out to have a double life, but Eduardo didn't know any of the details. Now he found himself curious and sympathetic. How did you explain something like that to your kids? How did you deal with it yourself?

And why on earth would anyone who was

married to Fiona have felt the need for someone else?

Eduardo did another walk-around, checked a couple of measurements and looked up costs online. By the time he'd finished, the afternoon sun was sinking toward the horizon.

Dinnertime. He needed to take a look at the carriage house, collect his kids and go back to the motel where they were staying. He'd finalize the estimate tonight and email it all to her, and mull over renting the carriage house if it seemed suitable. It would mean a late night, but the job would be great for his bottom line, and the fact that he could work on it basically from home, if the rental worked out, meant that he could get to it quickly.

Sofia was running across the lawn and he called to her. "Get your brother," he said. "I'm going to take a quick look at the carriage house and then go inside to talk to Mrs. Farmingham. After that, we'll head home."

"But we're having fun!"

"Sofia…" He lifted an eyebrow. She was just starting to question his authority, and he understood it was a stage. But she needed rules and boundaries, and she needed to obey.

"I…" She seemed to read the firmness in his eyes. "Okay." She gave him a little hug and then ran toward her brother.

Eduardo looked after her, bemused. How long would she keep giving him spontaneous hugs?

He walked through the carriage house. It was small but pretty and sturdy, well built. He checked the smoke alarms and found them all working. Three small bedrooms, a kitchen with space for a table, a sunny front room with hardwood floors.

If Fiona was charging a reasonable price, this place would be perfect.

He went to the front door of Fiona's house, tapped on it, and when there was no answer, he walked inside. "Fiona?"

He heard her voice from the kitchen, so he headed in that direction. "Hey, I'm about done—" He broke off, realizing she was on a video call.

The image on her big laptop computer screen was blurry, an older woman, but the voice was perfectly clear. "You really need to watch what you're eating, honey."

"Mom, we've talked about this." Fiona's voice was strained.

"But you've gained so much weight, and at your height…"

"Heard and understood, Mother. I'll get the kids." Fiona turned away, stepped out of the computer camera's range and buried her head in her hands. Her shoulders started to shake.

Eduardo backed away—nobody wanted a witness to their breakdown—but despite the fact that the old house had been beautifully renovated, you couldn't eliminate creaky floors. He felt the loose board beneath his feet at the same moment he heard a loud squeak.

Fiona looked up and saw him, and her face contorted even more. "Get out," she whispered through tears. "Just get out."

Chapter Three

"He has to hate me." Fiona pushed up the sleeves of her sweatshirt and picked up the pace, glancing over at her friends Susan and Daisy. She'd tried to back out of their planned morning walk, but they must have heard something in her voice, because they'd come over anyway and insisted that she join them. And they were right: it *did* feel good to get out and move in the fresh spring air.

"I doubt he *hates* you," Daisy said. "Okay, it sounds like it was awkward, and maybe you hurt his feelings, but Eduardo's an understanding guy." She looked slyly over at Fiona. "Handsome, too."

"Daisy!" Susan fake-punched her. "Remember what Pastor Ricky said last week. We need to focus on what's inside people, not what's outside. Although," she said, her voice thoughtful, "Eduardo *is* one of the best-looking workers at Hinton Enterprises. Almost as handsome as the boss."

"Biased much?" Daisy teased. "Sam's my brother, and I love him, but even I think judging a beauty contest between Eduardo and Sam would be a tough job."

"Would you guys stop?" Fiona dug in her pocket for a ponytail holder. "How Eduardo looks is the least of my worries. I kicked him out in a mean way after he'd come over to my house to make a landscaping estimate. I didn't even show him the carriage house. I'm an idiot." Her cheeks heated at the memory of looking up during her meltdown to see Eduardo's concerned face, of blurting out something, anything, to make him go away.

She'd regretted it only moments later, but by then he'd collected his kids and left. "I wasn't just rude to him. I disappointed and confused his kids, too. They were expecting to look at the carriage house. I'm sure he's decided to rent something else, now that he realizes what a loon I am."

"You're *not* a loon," Susan said. "You're a human being with emotions."

"Don't be so hard on yourself," Daisy added. "We all make mistakes."

"I guess."

Daisy squeezed her arm and Susan patted her

back, and the tightness in Fiona's chest relaxed just a little bit. A woman out weeding her garden called a greeting, and two mothers with babies in strollers waved from the other side of the street. In a fenced front yard, a toddler squatted to pet a puppy while his father talked on the phone.

Life went on.

"If it makes you feel any better, I'm the queen of saying the wrong thing, and most people forgive me for it," Susan added. "I'm sure Eduardo will forgive you if you apologize nicely."

"I can't apologize. I'm too embarrassed that he heard my mom calling me fat." Fiona could barely squeak the words out in front of her friends. "I mean, it's out there for everyone to see, but still…"

"You're not even close to fat!" Daisy sounded indignant.

"That's ridiculous," Susan said. "When you came to town, everyone talked about how you looked like a model. I was totally jealous when Sam's old mother-in-law tried to fix him up with you."

"I remember." Fiona thought back to that Fourth of July picnic almost two years ago. "I was such a mess then. Reggie had died earlier that year, and then I found out about his second family. I'd just moved here, and the kids were really struggling." She sighed. "But at least I was thin."

"Listen to yourself!" Susan scolded. "Would you trade where you are now for where you were back then, just to wear a smaller pants size? I mean, look at me." She patted her rounded stomach. "I've got baby weight I need to lose, sure, but I wouldn't trade it for the figure I used to have, no way."

"Of course you wouldn't." Daisy sounded just a little wistful. "And Sam wouldn't, either. He claims Sam Junior is the perfect child, and you're the perfect wife for producing him."

Susan snorted. "If he said *I* was perfect, he's delusional."

They reached Rescue River's small downtown and walked down Main Street. Early on a Monday morning, pedestrian traffic was light and most businesses were still closed. There was Mr. Love, though, sweeping the sidewalk in front of Love's Hardware, whistling a quiet tune. At eightysomething, he had more energy than most twenty-year-olds.

"Hey, Mr. Love," Daisy called.

The stooped dark-skinned man stopped sweeping and looked slightly to the left of them, leaning on his broom. "Who's that now? Is that you, Daisy Hinton?"

They came to a halt to chat with the man

whose visual impairment didn't stop him from doing anything and everything.

"Me, and Susan, and Fiona Farmingham. Do you know Fiona, Mr. Love?"

"Oh, we've met," the old man said before Fiona could answer. "I'm blessed to get a morning greeting from the three prettiest ladies in Rescue River. Excepting my Minnie, of course."

Daisy arched an eyebrow at Fiona and Susan. "Are you two finally out in the open?" she asked Mr. Love.

"Thinking about shopping for an engagement ring. At my age!" He shook his head, a big smile creasing his face. "God's been smiling on me in my golden years."

"That's wonderful news." Daisy gave him a gentle hug while Susan and Fiona offered their congratulations.

"Don't rush into congratulating me. She hasn't said yes." Mr. Love put a hand on Daisy's arm. "You listen to what I'm saying now. Life's short. Too short for avoiding love due to fear."

Daisy's cheeks went pink. "You're not giving me advice on my love life, are you?"

"My name *is* Love, after all," he said with a chuckle. "And at my age, I think I can claim a little wisdom. Now, you ladies get on. I know you've got more exercising to do on this fine day."

As they walked on through the downtown, the

old man's words echoed in Fiona's mind. Was *she* avoiding love due to fear?

Well…yeah. She was. But in her case, she had every reason to.

"Fiona! Listen to me." Susan glared at her.

"Sorry, I was spacing out," Fiona said. "What did I miss?"

"I was saying that it's important for those of us raising girls, especially, to help them grow up with a healthy body image."

"That's true," Fiona said, thinking of Susan's stepdaughter, Mindy, as well as her own three. "I wouldn't want to do to my girls what my mom does to me on a regular basis."

"Kids learn by example as much as by words," Susan said. "I've learned that during ten years of teaching elementary school. If you put yourself down in front of them, or if you're always on some crazy diet, they'll notice."

"Exactly," Daisy said. "Besides, some men like women who enjoy their food. Dion says—" She broke off, blushing.

Susan cocked her head. "Is there something you want to tell us, about you and the police chief?" she asked Daisy.

"No. Anyway, today isn't about me." Daisy turned away from Susan and looked at Fiona. "What are you going to do about Eduardo?"

What *was* she going to do? She couldn't let

the discomfort between them fester—if for no other reason than that they'd see each other at kids' events all the time. "I guess I could text him an apology."

"Text him? Really?" Daisy stepped in front of Fiona, making her stop. Susan came to her side, blocking Fiona's way.

"Call him?" Fiona asked weakly.

"God didn't give us a spirit of fear," Daisy said.

"And how about if you're offering a gift at the altar, and you remember someone is mad at you?" Susan added.

"Yes!" Daisy nodded vigorously. "The Bible doesn't say *text* them or *call* them. It says go to them."

"But that's because they didn't have that technology back then…" Fiona trailed off as her friends crossed their arms and shook their heads at the same time.

"Do I *have* to apologize in person?"

At that, Daisy and Susan turned to continue walking, each grabbing one of Fiona's arms. "Come on," Susan said. "We'll help you figure out what to say."

The next afternoon, Eduardo noticed two of the younger workers putting equipment away without doing the daily maintenance.

It would be easier to finish the jobs himself, but then the new guys wouldn't learn. "Tommy. Duke." He gestured toward the machinery the men had just put away. "You're not done."

"Man, don't you ever lighten up?" Duke grumbled good-naturedly as he grabbed a cloth and knelt beside the mower's grassy blades.

"He's got nothing else to do," Tommy joked. "He needs a social life. Good work there, my man," he added to Duke.

"That skid-steer loader you brought in needs its fluid levels checked," Eduardo said mildly.

"Sorry, man." Tommy turned toward the small vehicle and started the daily inspection. "I'm in a hurry. I've got to go get cleaned up and take my woman out on the town."

"On a Tuesday?"

"Anniversary," Tommy explained. "My aunt's taking the kids."

A warm band tightened around Eduardo's heart. He remembered the days when he'd scrambled to get a sitter, had scrimped and saved to take Elizabeth out for a special occasion. She'd argued against the expense, but she'd always given in and they'd had fun, usually ending the evening with dancing.

"Need the place swept out?" Tommy asked Eduardo.

"Nah, go on. Have fun. I'll finish up."

"Thanks!"

As the two men left, a text message buzzed, and Eduardo pulled his phone out of his pocket.

It's Fiona. Can you meet me at the Chatterbox?

Instead of answering, he started pushing a broom across the floor of the storage shed. What did she want to talk to him about? If she wanted to see the estimate on her landscaping job—even after she'd booted him out of her home—he supposed he should give it. But at the café? Why not at her house?

He pushed debris into a heap and looked for a dustpan. Another message buzzed.

My treat. I want to apologize.

No need to apologize, he texted back. But I can meet you and give you your estimate if you'd like.

Great. Half an hour?

See you there.

He pocketed his phone and tamped down the small surge of excitement in his chest. He liked Fiona, found her attractive, if the truth be told, but he wasn't sure about renting her carriage house. What if she decided to use it as an office again? Or decided to kick them out for reasons he couldn't understand, as she'd done the other night?

On the other hand, the situation at their little motel was deteriorating. After Diego and Sofia had spent several noisy hours kicking around a soccer ball outside yesterday, the manager had let Eduardo know that they couldn't stay much longer. "We just aren't set up for kids," the man had said apologetically. "Couple more days, fine, but I'd like to see you move on soon."

Which meant he needed to find another place today or tomorrow; easier said than done in the limited rental market of Rescue River.

Again, the thought of Fiona's carriage house came to mind.

Thirty minutes and one speed-shower later, Eduardo reached the Chatterbox. The place wasn't crowded midafternoon, and Fiona wasn't there yet.

He sat down at a table where he could watch the door, waving to a few coworkers from Hinton who were at the counter eating.

A moment later, Fiona flew into the restaurant, her purse swinging. He stood and she hurried over. "I'm sorry I was late!"

He glanced at the clock above the door as he

moved to pull out her chair. From the corner of his eye, he saw the Hinton workers nudging each other. One of them gave Eduardo a thumbs-up.

Heat rose in the back of his neck as he sat down across from her. "You're not late. I was early. Are you hungry?"

"I am, but I'm not going to get anything. Just coffee. You go ahead, though. It's my treat."

Not in this universe.

"Are you ready to order?" Their waiter arrived with an order pad.

"Coffee for both of us, and a piece of cherry pie for me," Eduardo said.

"Ice cream?"

"Absolutely," he said and looked at Fiona. "You're sure you don't want to join me?"

She bit her lip. "Well… No. No, thank you."

After their server walked away, Eduardo pulled out his tablet. "I have your estimate right here."

"Wait." Fiona touched his arm and then pulled her hand back. "I invited you here so I could apologize. I'm sorry I was so rude when you were at my house the other day."

"No need to apologize. We all have bad days." The question was did she make a practice of it? If she did, he probably shouldn't rely on renting her place.

"I was having a difficult conversation with my mother," she went on, "but that's no excuse. It wasn't your fault."

Ah. Mother-daughter issues. "No problem. Don't give it another thought. Should we talk about the estimate?"

"Yes, and the carriage house rental, too."

"Okay, sure." But he *wasn't* sure. He didn't think he wanted to move his family onto Fiona's property. She was a lovely lady, and kind, but was she reliable?

Unfortunately, though, he had no viable alternative.

He pulled out the tablet computer and started explaining his estimate for the landscaping job, crunching numbers, talking measurements, offering possibilities and alternatives based on price. Usually, the client was right with him on this kind of thing, but Fiona didn't seem to be paying attention. Was it because she was so wealthy she didn't care what she spent? Or was she not liking what he was proposing?

The third time she spaced out, he confronted her. "Look, would you rather I just give you the bottom line? Or are you uninterested? If you don't want to hire me, you can say it right out."

"Oh, no, it's not that!" Her hands twisted together in a washing motion. "I'm sorry, Eduardo. I just…" She trailed off.

"I'm in business. I know I'm not right for every potential client."

"I'm very interested. I'm just not good with numbers." She looked embarrassed.

Funny, he hadn't pegged Fiona as the ditzy careless type, but that was how she was acting. "No problem," he lied. He started from the beginning and went through it again, more slowly.

All the same, he lost her.

Something tickled at his brain, and before he could stop himself, he blurted it out. "Do you have something like dyslexia?"

"No!" She looked shocked. "Why would you even say that?"

"Sorry, crazy idea. It's just…" He trailed off and then shook his head. "I'm out of line. I shouldn't have said anything. I apologize."

She drew in a breath and visibly composed herself. "It's okay."

But it clearly wasn't, so he blundered on. "I just noticed… You're obviously a smart woman. But talking to you about math is a little bit like talking to my son, Diego, about letters and reading. He has dyslexia."

She let out a short harsh laugh. "I *wish* there was that kind of explanation for my weaknesses."

Compassion squeezed his heart as he studied her. She was wealthy and carefree on the surface, but there were layers upon layers to uncover in her, that much was clear.

Also, it was clear that he was a little too interested in exploring those layers.

"Here you go, sir." The waiter placed a large piece of cherry pie in front of him. Gooey, rich with fruit, the ice cream melting down the sides of the large triangle.

Fiona eyed it. "Wow, that looks delicious."

"Want a taste?" Without waiting for an answer, he cut her a small slice and slid it onto her saucer.

"I shouldn't, but…twist my arm." She took a tiny bite and her eyes widened. "This is fabulous!"

He felt absurdly happy to have given her something that brought her pleasure, however small.

"Let me look at the figures while you eat," she said. "Maybe I can get it through my thick skull."

He scrolled to the cover sheet and handed her the tablet. "That's the overview of what I'd recommend. I should've started with that, anyway, rather than bombarding you with a million details and choices."

She took another tiny bite of pie and smiled. "*So* good. Thank you." And then she focused on the tablet, frowning, asking the occasional question.

As he finished his pie, she nodded decisively. "I like what you've recommended. I'd be interested in hiring you if you're still willing."

"I'm willing and honored." Then his neck heated. *Honored?* That wasn't the kind of thing he'd normally say to a new client.

An elderly couple who'd been sitting at a table in the corner of the restaurant stood and headed toward the door. The white-haired woman used a walker, and the African American man who followed her held her shoulder. And they seemed to be arguing.

"Is that Mr. Love from the hardware store?" Eduardo asked, glad for a change of topic.

Fiona twisted to see, and then her face broke out in a smile. "Yes, and he's with Miss Minnie Falcon. I wonder…" She trailed off as the couple neared.

"I don't want to hear one more word about it," the woman said.

"Now, Minnie, don't shut me down cold. Hear me out."

Fiona stood and reached out a hand as the older couple started to pass by. "Miss Minnie. Mr. Love. It's nice to see you."

Eduardo stood, too, interested to see that Fiona was acquainted with the pair. He was grasping for signs that she was a good person to work for and rent from, and he needed to weigh the situation carefully. His kids deserved that.

"Well, well, is that Miss Fiona Farmingham?" Mr. Love asked.

"Yes, it is, and I'm with Eduardo Delgado, who works at Hinton. Do you both know him?"

"I certainly do," Mr. Love said. "I believe you stopped in two weeks ago for some crabgrass treatment, didn't you?"

"I'm impressed that you remember." Eduardo stepped closer, which brought him close enough to Fiona to notice that she was wearing perfume.

"Not all senior citizens are forgetful," the older woman said, her voice tart.

"Now, now, Minnie," Mr. Love soothed. "That's not what the young man meant."

"I was just surprised he remembered my order better than I did when he has so many customers," Eduardo said truthfully.

"Miss Minnie, have you met Eduardo Delgado?" Fiona asked, the tiniest hint of a smile in her voice. "He works at Hinton Enterprises."

"And he does some work at the Senior Towers. We've met," Miss Minnie said, "but the two of us can't stop to chat. We've seen quite enough of each other today, and our ride is waiting outside."

Mr. Love grasped Fiona's hand, then Eduardo's, smiling apologetically as Miss Minnie hurried him away.

Fiona sat back down, watching the two seniors depart. "I guess the marriage proposal didn't go well."

"They're contemplating marriage?" Wow. Amazing that two elderly people had that much faith in the future.

"Love is ageless, or so they say." She turned back to face him. "I don't suppose you were able to look at my carriage house the other day."

"I did take a look. It seems like a great place." He tried to keep his ambivalence from showing in his voice.

"It's cute. I love the front porch." She shrugged. "It's not much. It's small, but it's solid and clean."

"You'd mentioned before that you were using it for your business. Won't you need it for that again? Are you sure you want a tenant?"

"I might give entrepreneurship another go if… well, if I can get someone to help with the numbers part." She laughed self-deprecatingly, gesturing toward the tablet that had confused her. "But that won't happen for months. If ever."

"Then… I think we'll give the place a try."

"Great!" She smiled at him. "You can move in anytime. We'll deal with the lease then."

That smile was dazzling. Way too dazzling. "I have references if you'd like to check them."

She waved a hand. "I don't need references. I know you."

"Yeah, but you don't know whether I pay my bills."

She blushed. "I'm really not much of a businesswoman, am I?"

"Nothing wrong with being trusting."

Her expression darkened. "Believe me, there is."

The stories he'd heard about her husband came immediately to mind. How could a man have two separate families, deceiving both of them? What a jerk. Hard to fathom anyone so lacking in honor and morals.

The waiter brought their check, and Eduardo took it and reached for his wallet.

"I'll take that," she said. "It's on me." She fumbled in her purse.

"Fiona, I'm paying."

"No, really, it's no problem. I have plenty—"

Heat rose up the back of his neck. "I may not be at your level of affluence," he gritted out, "but I'm not going to let a lady pay the check." He extracted a bill and handed it to the server.

They both watched him walk away, not looking at each other.

"I'm sorry, Eduardo," she said after a moment, quietly. "I didn't mean to insult you."

And of course, she hadn't. It was just that he needed to keep in mind their relationship: landlord/tenant. Employer/employee. They lived on different planets, economically speaking.

And even if that barrier hadn't existed, he needed to remember how vulnerable Fiona was. She'd been hurt badly. She didn't need any more problems in her life.

Especially not a problem like him. Because despite her wealth—yeah, and her beauty, too— Fiona seemed like a woman who needed protection and support. And if he hadn't been able to provide that to Elizabeth, he definitely couldn't provide it to Fiona and her four kids.

Chapter Four

"Hey, Mom, they're here already!" Ryan burst into the kitchen, where Fiona was making Saturday-morning pancakes. "And they're carrying stuff inside. Can we help them move in?"

Maya slid off her chair and headed toward the window. Lauren shoved away her plate. "Can we, Mom?"

Fiona glanced up at the clock. Eight o'clock, a full hour before she'd expected Eduardo and his mover-friends to arrive. Briefly, she regretted her makeup-free face, ancient concert T-shirt and ripped jeans.

She went to stand behind Maya, looking out into the sunny yard. Sure enough, a midsize rental truck sat in front of the carriage house beside Eduardo's overloaded pickup. A couple of unfamiliar cars were parked along the edge of the alley road, and six or seven people milled around, along with Sofia and Diego.

Two men opened the back of the rental truck while another fumbled with the hinges of the carriage house's front door. Eduardo climbed into the back of the truck, then emerged a moment later holding a long metal ramp. He set it down, leaped nimbly to the ground and moved it so it made a walkway from the back of the truck. Diego and Sofia pulled boxes from the piled-high back of Eduardo's pickup.

Standing easily a head taller than the other men, Eduardo called out instructions as he moved to take a too-heavy box from Diego and steady a tall plant Sofia was carrying.

Even from here, Fiona could see his wide smile. Her mouth suddenly felt dry.

"Can we go out, Mom?" Now all three of her older kids clustered around the window.

Poppy banged her sippy cup on the table and pointed at her empty plate. "More pancakes first!"

Fiona clapped her hands. "Back to your seats, everyone." She hurried to the stove to flip pancakes that had gotten just a shade too brown. "We'll give the Delgados a chance to get started moving in. Once we've finished breakfast…"

The kids all started shoveling pancakes into their mouths.

"*...and* cleaned up, we'll stroll over there and see how they're doing. It looks like they have a lot of helpers, so maybe Sofia and Diego could come play here while the men work." She brought the last plate of pancakes to the table and sat down. She considered pouring herself a bowl of low-calorie cereal, but the pancakes smelled way too good.

Half an hour later, she followed the kids over to the carriage house. As they greeted Sofia and Diego, Eduardo approached her. Though the morning was still cool, sweat had gathered on his brow.

"We got started early," he said. "Hope we didn't wake you guys up. Some of the men have to work this afternoon."

"No, it's fine. We were up," she said. "In fact, the kids were ready to come out and offer their assistance the minute you pulled up. It's exciting for them."

"For us, too."

Diego and Ryan dodged in front of a pair of guys lifting a couch, and both Fiona and Eduardo spoke simultaneously with words of caution.

"Hey, careful there."

"Stay out of the men's way."

The men set the couch down in front of the carriage house's little porch and conferred, pointing at the door, obviously discussing how to get the couch inside.

"Come over here and meet my buddies," Eduardo said and started over toward the two men.

Fiona followed, feeling self-conscious in her Saturday-morning finest. She'd considered changing into better clothes, but that would have evoked notice from her kids. And she had to get used to the idea of being herself around Eduardo, who was, after all, renting her carriage house, not taking her out on a fancy date.

The men greeted her and one of them lifted an eyebrow and grinned, then said to Eduardo, "I see why you liked this place."

Eduardo opened his mouth, but before he could say anything, Fiona gave the man a wide vacuous smile. "Tim! I remember you. I've done some of the food banks with your wife."

"Right." The man's expression changed to bland friendliness.

"I'm Tony," said another man. "Pleased to meet you. I'd shake your hand, but mine's pretty dirty. I think I've seen you at the soccer field."

"That's right, you're Hailey and Kaylee's dad, aren't you?" The presence of another parent eased her discomfort.

"Hey, you guys letting me do all the work? How's that fair?" A young woman, pretty and muscular and dressed in Hinton groundskeeper garb, put down a box and marched over. "That's what you get, working with a bunch of guys," she said to Fiona with mock-disgust. "I'm Angie, and I'm guessing you and I could finish this move-in in half the time while these guys stand around shooting the breeze." She gave Eduardo a friendly nudge.

Fiona's senses went on high alert. Was Angie Eduardo's girlfriend?

And what business was *that* of Fiona's? Why did she care?

Angie grabbed the other two men's arms. "Come on, I don't know about you, but he's paying me by the hour. And not to stand around."

"Fine, fine." The others grumbled and left.

Which left her alone with Eduardo.

"Sorry about Tim," he said.

"I know him. It's not your fault. Look, how about if your kids come play at our house? They'd be out of your hair, and my kids would love it."

"That would be a huge help," he said gratefully. "Just while we're moving the big stuff. But, Fiona," he added as she started to turn, "I don't expect you to babysit my kids on a regular basis. It's a nice offer for today, but in the future, I'll either return the favor or keep the kids over here. That's not part of the contract."

"Um, okay." She felt unaccountably hurt. Was that what this was? A contract?

Late in the afternoon, Eduardo stretched as he watched the truck drive away. Between his friends and his coworkers, they'd finished the move on schedule. Not only that, but the beds were all set up and the furniture in place. Someone had even unpacked some of his kitchen boxes so there were dishes, pots and silverware ready to use. He sent up a prayer of thanks for the good people in his life.

Fiona being one of them now. She'd kept his kids busy and happy all day, fed them lunch and snacks, shown them kids' room decorating ideas on her computer. He had to be careful not to take advantage of her kindness, because she was obviously a caregiver to the core and great with kids. He grabbed his phone and called for pizza, enough for all of them.

Forty-five minutes later, he texted Fiona.

Pizza's on me. Come on over and bring your kids.

The kids consumed the pizza in record time, and the older four ran upstairs for the great task of room arrangement. Eduardo got the TV set up, and Fiona settled Maya and Poppy in front of a movie.

It was all very homey and too, too comfortable. Having Fiona and her kids here made Eduardo realize how lonely he'd been.

The problem was that in his loneliness there was the dangerous possibility he'd lead this wonderful woman on, make her think he was interested in a relationship when he wasn't. Or shouldn't be, anyway. He cast about for something to talk about, something serious and businesslike and impersonal.

It didn't take long for him to think of a safe topic. "Stay here," he said, "I found something in one of the closets."

A moment later he was back at the dining room table with a box in hand. "This was on the shelf in the room you said you were using for an office. Up high, pushed back. I took a peek and realized it might be important. Don't worry, I didn't read anything."

Fiona reached for the box with an expression of extreme distaste. "Is that what I think it is?" she murmured as she opened the lid.

Inside was a mess of receipts and envelopes and papers. "Ugh," she said as she shuffled through the papers aimlessly, then closed the lid. "Thanks for finding it."

"Sounds like you'd rather it had stayed lost."

"No," she said, "it's a good reminder, in case I ever get serious about starting another business. I can just pull this out and all those ideas will go away."

"That's from your business?" Eduardo tried to keep any kind of judgment out of his voice, but in truth, the jumble of paperwork horrified him. He thought of his own carefully organized spreadsheets, his neatly labeled file folders, the app he used to keep track of small receipts.

"Yeah." She sighed. "I... Well, like I mentioned, I'm not too great at math. Or at being organized. So I kept putting off getting the money side of things straightened out. That was one of the factors that led to the dog-walking business failing."

He nodded. "A lot of people hire a bookkeeper if numbers aren't their thing."

"I tried. She quit!" Fiona rolled her eyes. "I had too many kids, too much going on. I got overwhelmed and botched the details."

"Don't get down on yourself," he said, putting a hand over hers. "It's hard enough running a business with two kids, and I can't imagine doing it with four." Then, when his hand wanted to squeeze hers tighter, he pulled it back. *None of that*, he told himself sternly.

"Mama?" Poppy came over and leaned against Fiona's leg, and Fiona pulled her up onto her lap.

"How's it going, kiddo? Where's Maya?"

"She went upstairs." Poppy stuck her thumb

in her mouth, which seemed like a young thing for a three-year-old to do. But she was awfully cute. And she provided a good distraction, wiping the sadness off Fiona's face.

"I remember when Sofia was that age," he said. "And then Diego. They grow up so fast."

"I know. I want to cling on to my baby as long as I can. But she's getting big." As proof of that, Poppy wiggled hard to get down and started to slide to the floor.

Eduardo reached over and caught her, hands around her upper arms. "Careful there, young lady," he said, steadying her.

She wiggled away and grabbed Fiona's leg, looking back fearfully at Eduardo.

"I'm sorry." He looked from Poppy to Fiona. "I didn't realize..."

"She's not much used to men, that's all." She pulled Poppy up onto her lap. "Mr. Delgado is a very nice man."

Poppy shook her head. "Not nice."

Oh, great. Now Fiona would think there was something wrong with him. Because kids and dogs always know, right?

Fiona tapped Poppy's lips gently and shook her head. "We use kind words," she said and then reached out to Eduardo and patted his forearm. "She wasn't around her father much at all, and… Well, we were in a lot of turmoil shortly after she was born. It's had its impact."

"I understand. Diego went through a phase where he was nervous around strangers."

"I thought she'd have outgrown it by now." Fiona looked out the window, seeming to see something disturbing through the deepening twilight. Absently, she stroked Poppy's head until it rested against her chest. The little girl's eyes were barely able to stay open.

Eduardo wanted nothing more than to comfort Fiona, but that wasn't his place…was it?

He'd been fortunate enough to have a good marriage, with a wonderful woman. But he hadn't been able to keep her safe.

Yes, it had been bad timing. When the small landscaper he'd been working for had gone bankrupt, the minimal medical coverage he'd had for his family had been gone. It had taken time to get replacement coverage. To get a new job, too, what with a sick wife and two little kids. Once he'd finally found work, his new job had provided great benefits, even covering Elizabeth's preexisting condition. But the three-month gap had meant spotty treatment at a crucial stage of Elizabeth's illness, and although a couple of doctors had told him it wouldn't have made a difference, he knew better.

He'd never forget the feeling: three pairs of

eyes looking to him for protection and help he couldn't give.

He'd vowed after Elizabeth died that he would never marry again, never have more kids. His job was to take care of his own kids, raise them to adulthood in safety and security. *Not* to take on additional responsibilities he wouldn't be able to fulfill.

The fact that Fiona had her own money, could afford all the insurance and medical help she needed, didn't change one thing. Because challenges weren't only financial. There were all kinds of ways a man was supposed to take care of his family, and his confidence in his ability to do so had been broken.

He coughed and took a swig of soda, trying to wash away the depressing thoughts.

Fiona shifted the now-dozing Poppy to a more comfortable position and stroked her hair. "Sorry about that," she said.

"Sorry for what?"

"For spacing out on you. I got a little distracted, thinking about the past."

"Me, too," he admitted.

"Good thoughts?" She shifted Poppy against her shoulder. The little girl's eyes kept closing.

He shrugged. "Mostly. I had a wonderful marriage, but..."

"But what?"

"But I made mistakes." He looked into those caring eyes and felt a terrible urge to reveal everything. He even opened his mouth to do it, but he stopped himself.

"We all make mistakes," she said, glancing down at Poppy and then back at Eduardo. "I was a fool not to see what was going on with my husband. Maybe you've heard that he had a whole other family."

"I did hear that." He shook his head. "Must have been rotten."

"And we didn't find out until after he died. Do you know how frustrating that is?" Poppy raised her head, and Fiona bit her lip and started rocking and soothing her again. "There's no one to be mad at. No way for me to ask him all the questions I have. I'll never understand why he did what he did."

"Stinks." Again, Eduardo felt the urge to comfort her, to go over and put his arms around her. But aside from the fact that it would totally freak out little Poppy, it would be the mistake of starting something he couldn't finish.

"And you're not supposed to speak ill of the dead," she continued. "And anyway, I don't want the kids to grow up thinking there's something wrong with them because of what their father did. They already hear enough gossip and negativity from other kids."

"Even here in Rescue River?"

She leveled her hand and rocked it slightly back and forth in a so-so gesture. "A little. Not so much as back in Illinois, of course. And I hope that as we become more and more established in the community, people will judge us on the merits of what we are now, rather than on our history."

"I think they will. I, for one, already do."

Their eyes met and held just a second too long. Eduardo couldn't look away from that gorgeous face, disturbed with memories from the past.

She broke eye contact first. "Yeah, well, you're getting to see the worst of me. You can see firsthand the mess I made of my business." She looked down at the box of receipts. "And you can see me in my Saturday finest."

Fiona in her old jeans and T-shirt still looked incredible.

"Anyway," she said, touching his arm in a friendly way that burned right through him, "thanks for the pizza. I'm glad you guys are going to be living here."

"Speaking of living here, I'd better pull my home together and get my kids ready for bed." He stood, knowing it was abrupt and rude to push a guest out this way, but it was better than the alternative of pulling her into his arms, tiny sleeping darling and all.

* * *

On Monday morning, after getting the kids on the bus and dropping Poppy off at preschool—literally kicking and screaming—Fiona led Miss Minnie Falcon up the stairs of her porch and leaned her folding walker against the railing.

"Thank you for coming over," she said as she offered the older woman a comfortable rocking chair. "I needed the company."

"I could see that." Miss Minnie looked around appreciatively. "My, you have a lovely home, dear."

Fiona surveyed her sunny porch, satisfied that it was a bright, comfortable spot for people to gather. At the bottom of the steps, crocuses bloomed purple and gold. Chirping birds in the nearby apple trees created a lively chorus. "I'll get you some tea," she said and headed inside.

She hadn't been kidding about needing the company, not only because she worried about Poppy's separation anxiety but because Eduardo's truck was still in the driveway of the carriage house. She didn't know why he hadn't gone to work, but he was the last person she wanted to see.

They'd gotten a little too close on the day he'd moved in, or at least, it had felt like closeness to her. Apparently, he hadn't liked it, because he'd sent her and the kids away with an abruptness that wasn't like him. It had hurt, but she'd understood. Just because they were living on the same grounds didn't mean they should share every moment together. It was best not to get the kids into that pattern. So, yesterday, she'd hurried her kids out after church without even greeting Eduardo and his kids, and they'd done a day trip to a nearby nature reserve.

Now she finished making tea, put lemon and sugar on a tray and carried the lot out to the porch. Miss Minnie smiled as Fiona poured her a cup. "Now, this is nice," she said. "I've come to like living at the Senior Towers, but there are times when it's good to be in a real home."

"I was feeling blue when I ran into you at the church. You probably heard Poppy screaming. It's tough to walk away, even though everyone says preschool is good for her."

"The church preschool is wonderful," Miss Minnie declared. "And she's your fourth child. Surely, you know she's going to be okay."

Fiona stirred sugar into her own tea. "Poppy is different from the others. She's shy. Anxious."

"She'll grow out of it." Miss Minnie rocked gently. "You give her plenty of love. Opportunities to socialize, like the church preschool, are just what she needs."

"Do you think? She just started last month, three days per week. It's a battle to go every time, but the teachers say she settles down within fifteen minutes." Fiona shook her head. "My others were all eager to go to school and see their friends. Still are."

"Any idea why she's different?" The older woman studied her over the rim of her teacup, eyes piercing.

"It's my fault." Fiona sighed. "She must've picked up on my anxiety. I should have seen the signs sooner, but I was…going through a tough time." She picked up her tea and sipped it. "You probably know all about my family's history. Seems like everyone in Rescue River does."

Miss Minnie put down her cup with a little clatter. "Rise above it, young lady! You did nothing wrong."

"I suppose," Fiona said. "Still, after three years, I feel like an idiot for what happened."

"Because you were misled by a man?" Miss Minnie made a *pfft* sound. "We've all been there."

That surprised Fiona. "You, too?"

"Oh, my, yes." Miss Minnie rocked and looked out toward the road. "I thought I knew someone," she said, "and I didn't. My fiancé, to be exact."

"You were engaged?" Fiona was surprised, because Miss Minnie seemed like a confirmed and happy spinster.

Miss Minnie nodded but didn't offer more details. "We can all be fooled by love."

Seeing that she wanted to change the subject, Fiona obliged. "I'm bad at choosing. The last date I went on was a mess." She told Miss Minnie the story of her date with Henry and, to her surprise, she was able to make it funny enough that Miss Minnie laughed…and then Fiona did, too.

"Oh, my, the stories we get at the Senior Matchmakers. To say nothing of our own stories." Miss Minnie's face wrinkled with amusement. "Lou Ann Miller and her love triangle are the stuff of many a legend here in Rescue River."

The idea of the elders still going through romantic shenanigans gave Fiona an odd sort of hope. Maybe, when her kids were grown and she'd truly gotten over her past, she'd find love… or at least, have fun looking for it. "What about you?" she asked the older woman. "Any chance that you and Mr. Love might take your friendship to the next level?"

A blush crept up Miss Minnie's papery cheek and she waved a hand. "It would be so ridiculous at my age. To get engaged. To get married!"

"You volunteer at church and you started a business just last year," Fiona pointed out. "Age doesn't stop you in any other area. Why should it stop you from falling in love?"

"Oh, well." Miss Minnie rocked faster, her cheeks still pink.

"Nice to see you ladies taking advantage of this fine morning!" The deep male voice thrummed along Fiona's nerve endings as Eduardo approached and put down the bag of fertilizer he was carrying, wiping his forehead with a bandanna.

"I'm surprised you're not at work." Then Fiona felt her cheeks warm. She didn't want Eduardo to think she was keeping track of his movements.

Miss Minnie's sharp, observant eyes flashed from one face to the other. "Yes, indeed. Mr. Sam Hinton can barely run Hinton Enterprises without you from what I hear."

Eduardo's already-tan skin went a shade darker. "Not the case. I keep the outside of the property running so Sam can do the hard stuff inside. And the folks on my shift are pretty well trained. They get along just fine when I'm not there to supervise."

"I'm sure. Sam speaks highly of your teaching abilities, too."

Fiona studied him with interest. She'd known he was a supervisor, but Miss Minnie was making it sound like he headed the entire grounds operations. Most men tended to brag about their work, but Eduardo was always humble.

"Thank you for telling me that, Miss Minnie,"

he said now and then looked at Fiona. "I'm taking the day off to get the house in order, but I'd also like to get a start on your garden project if that's okay with you."

"Of course, that would be wonderful."

"I'm planning to dig out the grass where the raised bed will go. That'll help drainage and weed control. And then sometime this week, I'll pick up the boards to build the terrace walls. Sound good?"

"Perfect." She watched him walk away, noticing the way the sun shone on his dark hair.

When she came back to herself, Miss Minnie was looking at her, one eyebrow lifted.

"So it's like that, is it?" the older woman asked.

"Like what?" What had Miss Minnie seen in her expression? Had Eduardo seen the same thing, now or earlier? Was that why he'd kicked them out of the carriage house on Saturday?

Miss Minnie was still studying her and she didn't answer Fiona's question. "Do you have a Bible?" she asked unexpectedly.

"Of course!"

"Would you get it, please?"

"Um, sure." She stood and headed into the house. What was *this* all about? Miss Minnie was, after all, a Sunday school teacher from way back. But Fiona, discombobulated as she was by Eduardo's presence, didn't feel like being preached at.

She schooled her expression before returning to the porch and handing Miss Minnie her Good News Bible. Miss Minnie ran her hands over the cover. "I love this translation," she said. "And I think it has something to say to both of us." She flipped the pages with the ease of long familiarity and then ran a weathered finger down a page. "Ah, here we are. Second Corinthians 5:17. Do you know it?" She looked up at Fiona expectantly.

"I'm sorry. I don't." Fiona felt inadequate.

"I'm going to read it to you," Miss Minnie said, her voice taking on a teacher's firm tone. "Verse 17: 'Old things are passed away; behold, all things are become new.' In other words, anyone who is joined to Christ is a new creation." She looked up at Fiona.

Fiona nodded, processing the words.

"Sit down, dear. I have the sense that you're focusing on the past and what went wrong in it. With your children, Poppy in particular. And that it's hindering any possible connection with that handsome young man there."

"Eduardo isn't interested—" She stopped. "Anyway, I *did* make huge mistakes in the past."

Miss Minnie held up a hand. "The point is, you're joined to Christ, and you're a new creation. You can put all that behind you. The old is gone, and the new has come." Her face broke into a crinkly smile.

Fiona couldn't help smiling back. "If it's true for me, Miss Minnie, then it's true for you, isn't it? You need to open your mind to all the new possibilities ahead of you."

Miss Minnie's smile went wry. "So a certain gentleman keeps telling me," she said.

As if on cue, a sedan pulled up. "I believe that's my ride," Miss Minnie said, color blooming in her cheeks.

Mr. Love got out of the passenger's side, and a younger woman emerged from the driver's seat. "That's his granddaughter," Miss Minnie said. "Could you help me up, dear? She claims she's driving him around as a charitable act, but I suspect she wants to keep an eye on us as well."

"Keeping you out of trouble?" Fiona couldn't help smiling as she helped the older woman down the stairs and unfolded her walker for her.

"And rightly so," Miss Minnie said tartly as she made her way down the sidewalk. "Men never change. Thank you for the tea and conversation, dear. You think about what we discussed."

"I will." Fiona watched as Mr. Love helped Minnie into the back seat and then climbed in beside her.

"Is it any wonder I feel like a chauffeur?" the granddaughter asked with good-natured exasperation. With a wave and a honk, they were off.

Fiona checked the time. Another hour and a half before she had to pick up Poppy. And there was Eduardo, working up a sweat, creating the garden of her dreams.

She grabbed a pair of gloves and a shovel from the shed and approached him. "Need a hand?" she asked. "I hate to sit and watch while you're slaving away."

He stopped, leaning on his shovel. "Truthfully? No."

She'd already lifted her shovel to start digging. She froze in midair and looked at him. "How come?"

"You hired me to do the job. If you're going to be uncomfortable with me working for you, we should call it off right now."

"I didn't say I was uncomfortable with you working for me," she said, although she kind of *had* said that. "I said I wanted to help. Does that make *you* uncomfortable?"

He hesitated and then looked away across the yard, still leaning on his shovel. Which gave Fiona the time to analyze his answer and come up with the unpleasant truth.

"Look," she said, "if you don't want me to help, if it's too much togetherness, that's fine. I didn't even consider that you might enjoy having your day off to work by yourself, without having to talk to someone else all the time." She was babbling. Totally babbling, because she felt so mortified and embarrassed to have forced herself on him.

What was that Bible verse Miss Minnie had insisted on reading to her? Something about how she was a new creation.

She wasn't the same person who'd been betrayed, rejected and made to look ridiculous by a man who had vowed to cherish her. No, she'd grown beyond that...sort of.

But that still didn't make her the type of woman most men wanted to spend time with. She pulled off her gardening gloves and turned away.

A hand on her shoulder stopped her. "Fiona." Eduardo's voice was closer than she expected behind her. "It's not that I don't want to be with you."

She half turned back, not meeting his eyes. "It isn't?"

"No," he said, "it's that I want to be with you too much."

"You don't have to say that, Eduardo. I'll get out of your hair." And she hurried off toward the house, before he could say more painfully kind but empty things.

Chapter Five

❧

The next Saturday, Eduardo was washing dishes when Sofia and Diego burst into the carriage house. "Dad!" Diego cried. "Lauren and Ryan and Maya and Poppy got a dog!"

Eduardo turned, his hands soapy, as both of his kids crashed into him. "Hey, slow down."

"It's a hound-pointer mix, like, *this* big." Sofia held her hands a yardstick apart.

"They got him at A Dog's Last Chance and his name is Brownie, 'cause he's mostly brown!"

"He has the softest floppy ears," Sofia said. "Come out and see!"

Their excitement made him smile. "You go ahead. I'll be right out."

"Hurry!" They rushed outside, letting the screen door slam.

Eduardo rinsed the last of the dishes and dried his hands. If he had any sense, he'd stay inside and ignore the feelings that roiled in his chest whenever he thought of the family across the yard. Particularly the family's mother.

He needed to focus on work and his own kids, like he'd been doing for the past week, ever since he'd made his idiotic pronouncement about wanting Fiona around too much.

Why had he gone and done such a foolish thing?

Because he *didn't* have any sense, obviously. And because it was the truth.

But it also had to do with the vulnerability in her eyes as she'd said he probably didn't want her around. He couldn't let her keep assuming that, putting herself down, believing that all men were like her ridiculous, deluded husband who'd betrayed her.

Except who had appointed him caretaker of the world? He was the *worst* candidate for that job.

Maybe Fiona wouldn't be outside with her kids. Maybe he could come out and meet the new pup and skulk back inside without encountering the tall redheaded beauty who'd been haunting his dreams.

But of course, that wasn't how it played out. When he crossed the lawn to the side yard near Fiona's house, she was right there on the ground with her kids and an ecstatic brown-and-white hound, who was bounding from one kid to the next, barking madly.

She glanced up at him, gave a brief wave and then focused on the dog. "Ryan, let your sister have a turn," she said to her son, who'd grabbed the new dog by the collar.

Maya scooted over and wrapped her arms around the dog's neck, fearlessly, and stuck out her tongue at her brother.

"Poppy needs a turn, too," Lauren said, looking up at her mother for approval, as the dog bounded away again.

"That's a kind thought, Lauren." Fiona brushed a hand over her daughter's reddish-brown hair. "But I'm not sure Poppy wants a turn just yet."

"Yes, she does! C'mere, Brownie!" Ryan had knelt beside Poppy, and Maya ran to squat on her little sister's other side.

Gamely, the dog bounded their way, placed oversize paws on Poppy's lap and proceeded to lick her face.

Poppy jerked back and wailed.

In a flash, Fiona was there, picking Poppy up and frowning at Ryan and Maya. "We never force people to play with the dog. You know it takes your sister some time to warm up."

"Aw, Mom, she liked him at the farm," Ryan said.

Fiona just raised an eyebrow at him, holding Poppy on her hip and stroking her hair.

"I'm sorry, Pop," Ryan said.

"Me, too. C'mon, let's throw a ball for him!" Maya matched word to action, grabbing a ball and throwing it surprisingly far for a child her age.

All three of Fiona's older kids, plus Eduardo's two, ran after the dog, leaving Fiona, Eduardo and Poppy to watch.

Eduardo blew out a sigh and tried not to notice the way the sun set fire to Fiona's hair. Or the curve of her smile as she watched her kids play. Or the unconsciously warm and motherly way she made little sounds in her throat to soothe her youngest, who still rested her head on Fiona's shoulder.

He didn't want to notice what a deep-down good person Fiona was. But being around her so much made that reality impossible to ignore.

Maybe he needed to start looking for a new place to live. Before he did something crazy again, such as tell her how much he liked being around her.

"Five more minutes, kids," she called, clearly oblivious to his inner turmoil. Then she turned to him. "I told them they needed to let him rest today. Even though he's having a good time, making a move is stressful on an animal. He's not used to this kind of craziness."

"He sure is cute." There. That was an innocuous comment anyone would make, right?

Abruptly, the kids' voices rose in unhappy tones, shouting back and forth. "Uh-oh," Fiona said, and they both started walking toward the noise.

Around the corner of the house, Fiona's kids knelt, holding the dog.

Eduardo's two stood shoulder to shoulder six feet away, faces stormy.

"He's *our* dog!" Lauren was saying.

"We *know* that, but you could at least let us pet him."

Ryan squeezed the dog against his chest. "You don't know how to take care of a dog like we do."

"Oh, like you have *all this* experience with dogs," Sofia said cuttingly. "You only got one this morning."

Maya sat on the ground and wrapped her arms around the dog, half tugging it out of Ryan's lap. The dog responded with a plaintive yelp.

Fiona marched over to her kids and Eduardo to his. Behind him, Eduardo heard Fiona remonstrating.

"They're being selfish, Dad." Diego was almost crying. "I just want to play with him. I wasn't trying to steal him."

"He's an ugly dog, anyway," Sofia said, just loud enough to set off another wave of outrage among Fiona's kids. "And he runs around like he's crazy."

"Hey." Eduardo knelt and gripped a forearm of each of them, not tight, but firm, so they couldn't escape. "When our friends get something new, we celebrate with them. We don't try to take it away." He frowned at Sofia. "And we don't talk it down. That's unkind and it's uncalled for."

"I'm sorry," Sofia said, looking away.

"I'm not the one you need to apologize to."

She pressed her lips together and glared at Eduardo.

He glared right back.

She yanked her arm out of his grip and crossed her arms over her chest. "Sorry," she yelled over toward the Farmingham kids. Then she spun and ran toward the house.

"I'm sorry, Dad," Diego said, sounding much more sincere than his sister. "Can I go tell them?"

"First tell me how you're going to act toward the new dog."

"I'm going to watch him and talk to him and only pet him if they say I can."

"And not argue?"

"Yeah." Diego was practically bouncing, looking over at the four kids, who were sitting around their mother while she held the dog at her side and patted it gently.

"Go ahead," he said.

Eduardo watched as Diego approached the

Farminghams, said something and was welcomed to join the little group. A minute later, Lauren ran toward the carriage house, where Sofia had disappeared.

Eduardo busied himself pulling a few early weeds, keeping his ear tuned toward his place for any signs of an argument. But a few minutes later, Lauren came back out with Sofia, the two of them talking like old friends. And the next minute, all six kids were running and playing with the dog and each other.

"Disaster averted," Fiona said, coming to stand beside Eduardo. "I'm sorry. I should have warned you we were getting a dog, but this little trip came up suddenly. Once we were there, seeing all the dogs who needed homes…" She shrugged and lifted her hands. "What can I say, I'm a sucker for big brown eyes." Then she looked at him and clapped a hand over her mouth.

Eduardo couldn't resist smiling a little, enjoying the way her cheeks were going pink. Of course, she hadn't meant anything by it. No way had she been flirting with him. She wasn't the type.

"I didn't mean… I meant, a *dog's* brown eyes… Oh, wow. I'd better stop talking."

"No, don't worry. I understand. I didn't think you meant anything." Wasn't there some yard work he could do, rather than trying to hold an intelligible conversation with the most gorgeous woman he'd ever seen?

The unbidden thought shocked him. Was Fiona more gorgeous than Elizabeth had been?

Guilt rose, but he firmly tamped it down. Every woman was beautiful in her own way; he truly believed that. Elizabeth had been, and Fiona was.

It was just that Fiona was right here, smelling like hyacinths…

"Hey, Dad!"

"Mom!"

The six kids came running toward them, Lauren carrying Poppy, the dog bounding alongside. "We want to talk to you," Sofia said, offering him a winning smile.

"Okay." Eduardo could tell some kind of con job was coming, but he still welcomed the interruption.

"Families are important, right?" Sofia said.

"Yes, of course," Eduardo said, cocking his head to one side and looking skeptically at his daughter.

"And it's important to be with your family, to be all together," Diego said. "That's why we go visit Mexico sometimes."

"Right."

"But *this* dog—" Sofia indicated Brownie "—this dog was taken away from his mother."

Eduardo frowned. "He's not a little puppy. It's okay for him to be taken away."

"But, Dad, Brownie's mom is still at A Dog's Last Chance," Diego said. "And she was really sad to be left behind. Right?" He turned, and all four Farmingham kids nodded solemnly. Even the dog seemed to agree, eyes fixed on Eduardo, tongue lolling.

"And she's old, Mr. Delgado," Ryan said. "She has grey hair on her nose."

Eduardo was starting to see where this was going. Automatically, he shook his head.

"So we were wondering…" Diego started and trailed off.

Sofia put a hand on her brother's shoulder. "Could *we* get Brownie's mother and have her be our dog?"

"No." Eduardo drew in a breath. "No, we're not ready for a dog."

"Aww, Dad!" Diego's face crinkled into a pout.

"Come on, my kids," Fiona said. "Lunchtime, and time for Brownie to have a rest."

The kids complained, but they did as Fiona said. She gave him a little wave and a rueful look—perhaps an apology for stirring up his kids' desire for a dog—and then followed them toward her house.

She didn't invite them to join in. Not that he wanted to, not that he would have, but he noticed the omission because she was usually quick to offer hospitality.

She was guarded around him now. As well she should be, but it was hard. "Go on inside," he told his sulky kids. "I'll be along in a minute. I need to pull the rest of these weeds." In reality, he needed to collect his thoughts before entering into the get-a-dog fray.

When he did go inside, the kids were already pulling peanut butter and jelly out of the cupboard and arguing. He started into the kitchen to break it up and then heard what they were saying and froze.

"That wasn't why she died, Diego. It didn't have anything to do with you knocking over that lamp."

Diego didn't speak. His head was bowed over the sandwich he was making.

"*I'm* the one who made her sicker. I wanted her to come to school like the other moms, and she didn't, and I yelled at her about it. She went to the hospital the next day, and she never came home."

A tight band circled Eduardo's chest and squeezed tight. He hadn't known his kids still felt guilty about Elizabeth's death. The concerns they'd raised had been addressed long ago, or so he'd thought. But maybe, unintentionally, he'd brushed them aside.

Just like the doctors had brushed aside his own feelings of guilt about not having good insurance when Elizabeth had first gotten sick.

He hadn't just said "Oh, okay" and dropped his own guilt instantly. Why would he expect that his kids could do that?

He came up behind his son and daughter, who were facing the counter, and put a hand on each shoulder. Leaned close and inhaled the sweaty-kid smell of their hair. "Mom died because she had cancer," he said firmly. "Not because of anything you did."

Two pairs of hands froze in their work, then started up again. "We know, Dad," Sofia said.

"But from what I heard you both say," he persisted, "it sounds like you're still blaming yourselves."

Diego looked up at him. "I know you said it's not my fault, but I wish I didn't break the lamp. I remember she yelled at me, and then she cried. And before that, people were always telling me to be quiet and not upset Mom. So when I did…"

Eduardo shook his head and pulled Diego to him, enveloping him in a hug that was as much for himself as for his son. He reached out his other hand and pulled Sofia into the embrace. "Kids are supposed to be kids," he explained. "She knew that you were young, and she wanted you to have fun and play. She knew things could break."

"But she cried," Diego said.

"And she cried when I yelled at her," Sofia added. "Her face got really red."

Eduardo pulled them over to the kitchen table and sat them down in their chairs, then knelt between them. "It's true she got upset sometimes," he said. "Because Mom was a real human being, with real feelings. She cried a lot toward the end because..." He swallowed the tight knot in his throat. "Because she knew she didn't have much time left with us. She knew how sick she was long before you broke the lamp and yelled at her. It made her sad. Mad, even, sometimes."

"I was mad at her," Sofia said cautiously, "when she didn't come to Muffins-for-Moms day. I told her about it, but she forgot. How could she forget?"

Eduardo sighed. "The drugs the doctors gave her made her forget things sometimes. But you know what? I should have remembered Muffins-for-Moms, but I forgot, too." He should have found a friend or relative to attend, but life had been so crazy at that awful time. "The thing is... I'm not perfect and neither was Mom. And you don't have to be perfect, either. Everybody makes mistakes."

"And everybody sins," Diego said thoughtfully. "We talked about it in Sunday school, and kids told what they'd done wrong. But I made something up, because I didn't want to tell about the lamp." Tears stood in his brown eyes, and his concerned expression was the exact replica of his mother's. The sight made Eduardo's own eyes burn.

"Breaking the lamp wasn't even a sin, Diego. It was just an accident," Sofia said. "But me yelling at her was a sin."

Eduardo swallowed. One was never ready for these big discussions with kids. They came suddenly, over peanut butter sandwiches on a Saturday afternoon, and they just had to be handled as best as possible. "Feelings are feelings," he told Sofia. "They're not right or wrong. It was okay to feel mad at Mom for forgetting. Even for being sick."

Both kids' heads snapped around to stare at him.

Ah. That was the core, then. "Sometimes," he told them, "I felt angry at Mom for being sick. I wished she could have fun and do things like she used to do." The admission made him ashamed, but he could see that his kids were eating up every word. "Sometimes, she got mad at me for being so healthy, I think."

"Did she get mad at us for that?" Sofia asked.

"No," he said, filling his voice with the certainty that he felt. "The most she ever got was annoyed with you for the same things parents always get annoyed about. She loved you both so much, and she was glad you were healthy and strong. Her biggest hope was to get to see you grow up, to be your mom and do everything moms do." His throat closed then, and he couldn't say any more. He just pulled them both close and held them until he could get himself under control.

Showing emotions was okay—good, even; that was what the social worker and the grief counselor had said right after Elizabeth's death. But still, he had to be strong for his kids. Had to be their rock. They needed to know that he wouldn't fall apart on them.

So he drew in a deep breath, then another, and then he pulled back from them and stood. They both looked at him, eyes round and teary and serious.

"I'm pretty hungry," he lied. "I'm hoping you made one of those sandwiches for me."

"We did, Dad," Diego said. "The one with the most jelly, because—"

Sofia slapped a hand over her brother's mouth

and glared at him. "Just sit down, Daddy, and we'll bring you a sandwich and milk."

Which meant they were still trying to butter him up about the dog. But after the conversation they'd just had, arguing about a dog seemed so simple and happy and normal. He had to be careful, or he'd let himself make an emotional decision that wouldn't be good for any of them. Something he seemed to be tempted to do a lot of these days, he thought, looking over at Fiona's house.

He had to be careful about her, too. Because given his history, the way he'd failed Elizabeth and the long-lasting repercussions for his kids, getting too close to Fiona would put both her *and* her kids at risk.

Chapter Six

~🦢~

The next day, after they'd all changed out of their church clothes, Fiona and the kids got in the car and headed for the park. Brownie bounced from one side of the middle seat to the other, trying to get his head out the window, his long brown ears blowing in the breeze. The kids weren't bickering, the day was bright and sunny, and Fiona's strange feelings about Eduardo had settled down.

"Wasn't this a good idea, Mom?" Lauren asked as she helped Fiona pull out the picnic basket, a blanket and a bunch of yard toys.

Poppy squatted down to examine a dandelion. Maya grabbed Brownie's leash and took off across the field, Ryan chasing behind.

"Yes, honey, good idea. Hey, kids, back here right now!" Fiona called after her middle two.

Poppy tugged at Fiona's leg. "Look, Mommy,

it's a lion flower!" she crowed, holding up a dandelion. "Cuz it's like a lion's mane, right?"

Fiona's heart tugged and she shared a smile with Lauren as she bent down and picked Poppy up, settling her on her hip. Nothing was as sweet as a small child's view of the world. She wanted to hold her youngest tight and beg her to stay little.

Ryan jogged back, Maya and Brownie trailing behind. Fiona waited until all the kids clustered around her. "Okay, first rule—Brownie stays on the leash all the time, and you hold him with your hand through the strap like they showed us out at the rescue farm. Understand?"

They all nodded quickly.

"Second—before you play, everyone helps carry stuff to the picnic table. Maya, you're on toys. Ryan, the picnic basket. Lauren, you're going to help me carry the cooler, and I want you to hold Brownie's leash."

Sighs and groans.

"I wanna help, too," Poppy protested.

"I need you to carry the..." Fiona looked around.

"This Frisbee, because it's a little bit broken and you have to be careful with it." Maya reached into a basket and produced a Frisbee with a tiny flaw on the side. She handed it to Poppy. "Be careful, okay?"

"Okay!" Still in Fiona's arms, Poppy nodded seriously and held the Frisbee as if it were made of delicate glass.

Fiona smiled her thanks at Maya. She loved it when the kids were sweet with each other. *They really were obedient and helpful a lot of the time,* she thought gratefully as everyone picked up their assigned items. She turned toward their usual table.

"Can we have our picnic over there instead?" Ryan pointed toward a cluster of tables near the park's north side.

"Well...it's a little farther from the playground."

"But there's more room for Brownie to run," Lauren pointed out.

"And we're tired of going to the same picnic table all the time," Ryan added.

"Yeah, let's do something new." Lauren smiled brightly as she picked up her side of the cooler.

Fiona narrowed her eyes as she looked from the suggested spot to her two eldest kids. Something told her they'd agreed on this location change beforehand. The only question was why.

"Let's go *somewhere*! I want to play!" Maya jumped up and down, the Frisbees and balls bouncing in her basket.

"Please, Mom?" Lauren begged. "I'm tired of sitting by the little kids' playground."

"What do you think, Miss Poppy?" Fiona asked, rubbing noses with her youngest until she giggled.

"I'll give you piggyback rides and let you have my cookie," Lauren said.

"Yay!"

More and more suspicious. But Fiona couldn't think of a reason *not* to set up in a different section of Rescue River's large downtown park, so she nodded consent and followed her excited kids to the cluster of picnic tables they'd chosen. The distant sound of barking dogs gave her a moment's concern, but Lauren had Brownie tight on his leash, and the dog was too engrossed in sniffing every tree and chasing every butterfly to give the faraway dogs any notice.

"Put your basket by that tree," she directed Maya, "and then you can go play. Stay where you can see me, though."

"I will, Mom." Maya dropped the basket of toys and took off toward a couple of girls Fiona recognized from her school.

Ryan placed the food basket carefully on the table. "Do you want me to help get things out?" He glanced longingly toward an apple tree with low sturdy branches.

"No, it's okay," Fiona said. "Go climb. You, too, honey," she said to Lauren. "Go play. Just keep an eye on your sister."

"I will. Come on, Poppy." Lauren took her little sister's hand and they headed off across the grass.

As Fiona spread the tablecloth and started pulling out potato salad and plastic-wrapped sandwiches, the sound of barking caught her attention again, louder and closer this time.

"Hey, Fiona!" Troy Hinton's booming voice rang out behind her. "Coming back for more?"

She turned to see the tall veterinarian and shelter manager carrying a crate with a small terrier inside, yapping madly. In his other hand, upside down, was a sign that said *A Dog's Best Friend: Animal Rescue... A Day in the Park*.

Troy reached her side and set down the small dog's crate on the picnic table beside hers. "How's Brownie working out?" he asked.

"We love him. The kids are over there playing with him right now. What's..." She waved her hand toward the small dog, the sign and the two other workers she now saw headed in their general direction, with large dogs pulling at their leashes.

"It's our annual adoption-day-in-the-park. We like to get the dogs out in front of the public, see if we can find homes for some of the hard-to-place ones."

"Nice," she said, beginning to see the plan

behind her kids' insistence on coming to this side of the park.

"Stop over if you get a chance. Angelica's coming later, with the kids, and she'd love to see you." He grabbed the crate and walked over toward a young volunteer who was practically being dragged along by a large boxer.

Fiona pulled drinks out of the cooler and put them on the edges of the tablecloth to weigh it down. If the kids thought she'd get another dog for them, they were out of their collective minds. She'd been very clear about that, and given how high-energy Brownie was, she'd been right. No way could they handle more than one. She wasn't going to give in to their ganging up on her.

"Fiona?"

She turned, and the sight of Eduardo sent a peculiar sensation down her spine. She turned, reclosable bag of chocolate chip cookies in hand. "Eduardo? What are you…" She stopped herself. He had every right to come to the park, but…

He glanced around at her picnic supplies and then back at her. He frowned. "Did your kids suggest coming today?"

She nodded slowly. "And they insisted we sit over here. Right by where Troy Hinton's setting up his adopt-a-dog event."

Eduardo scrubbed a hand over his face. "My kids begged me to bring our lunch here, too.

They've been on me all morning, trying to talk me into getting a dog."

She pushed out a laugh. "Sorry about that. When we brought Brownie home, I wasn't thinking about the pressure it would create for you."

He shrugged. "Not your fault. You can't run your family life based on not upsetting mine."

"True, but… I'm still sorry." She shaded her eyes to look over toward the dog rescue setup. Sure enough, her own kids and Eduardo's—along with a few others—were clustering around the caged and leashed adoptable dogs. Brownie bounced around hysterically barking, almost pulling Maya off her feet.

"I'd better go over there," she said. "I don't know what my kids are thinking. We already have all the dog we can handle."

"I think I might have an inkling," Eduardo said. "I'll come along, too, if you don't mind."

Eduardo's presence distracted Fiona from her annoyance with her kids. It was nice to walk beside a man several inches taller than she was. She didn't feel like a giant, as she sometimes did. It would be easy for him to put his arm around her. She'd actually fit beneath his shoulder.

And then she caught herself. Was she seriously daydreaming about cuddling up to Eduardo? That was about as smart as standing in front of the bakery window when you were dieting. She couldn't have a man like Eduardo, and there was no use torturing herself by imagining she could.

Except it was hard to resist her feelings. When his kids spotted them coming and ran over, he reached out muscular arms and caught one in each, kneeling down to mock-bang their heads together. His teeth flashed white in his deeply tanned face, and the care and fun in his eyes took her breath away. His kids seemed to know how special they had it, too; they both clung onto him for an extra few seconds, their love for their father obvious. For a moment, she ached at the thought that her own children had no such manly protector.

Ryan ran toward the trio and then stopped a few feet away from them, watching until the group hug broke up. His face held a mix of longing and jealousy. Of course, he was getting to the age where a mom wasn't enough. He needed a father figure, and Fiona was going to work on it. Maybe the husbands of some of her friends—Susan Hinton, Fern from the library—would be willing to spend a little male bonding time with Ryan. Or maybe it was time to get him into Boy Scouts, something he could do without his sisters always nearby.

"Dad, you gotta come see this!" Diego tugged

at his father's hand, and a moment later, Ryan joined in. "Yeah, Mr. Delgado, come and see!"

The two boys pulled him toward the dogs and he let them, flashing an eye roll Fiona's way.

Sofia looked up at Fiona. "Do you want to come, too?" she asked hesitantly. "It's Brownie's mother who's here today. We hope Dad will let us get her."

Fiona didn't want to condone the behind-the-scenes manipulation that had obviously gone on between the kids. But the little wrinkle between Sofia's brows, the plaintive expression on her face, touched Fiona's heart. "I'll come look," she said. "But your dad will have to make the decision that's right for your family."

"I know." Sofia walked beside her. "He will. He'll pray about it."

Fiona smiled and impulsively ran a hand over Sofia's hair. "That's what I did, too."

"And God told you to get a dog?" Sofia reached up and took Fiona's hand, her eyes full of hope.

The affectionate gesture from the motherless little girl tugged at Fiona's heartstrings. "Not exactly. But I got a sense of peace about it, like if the right dog was there we'd know it, and we'd know if we were ready to handle the responsibility."

"And then you got Brownie!" Sofia took an

extra skip, still clinging to Fiona. "I hope we can get Brownie's mom. I think our mom would have wanted us to."

"Really?" Fiona wondered whether that was true. "What's the dog's name? I don't think I met her at the shelter. I was too busy filling out paperwork for Brownie."

"She's called Sparkles." The little girl looked up at Fiona. "She had cancer, like my mom, but she didn't die from it. She just had to have her leg taken off, but she's still really pretty and nice. And I think—" She broke off.

Fiona swallowed the sudden lump in her throat. "What, honey?"

"I think she'd like to be with her son, Brownie. Just like our mom would like to be with us, if she could."

They were approaching the raucous collection of dogs and kids, so Fiona was spared having to answer. But her heart twisted into an impossible knot.

Of course, given Sofia's logic, she wanted the Delgado kids to get Brownie's mother. Except that the Delgado's residence near her own wasn't going to last forever. The kids and the dogs would be separated, maybe in a month, maybe several. They had to be careful about mingling their families, tightening the connections between them.

Eduardo's sweet children had already endured a terrible loss. Her own kids had as well.

Letting them get closer, having them share pets in common and become better friends, was a risk to young hearts that had already been broken.

Not to mention the risk to her own heart.

That evening, Eduardo sat outside on the grass, warm in the setting sun, watching his two kids and Fiona's four play with Brownie and Sparkles.

The grey-muzzled mama dog barked from a seated position, and Brownie kept bounding in circles around his mother. When he got close enough, she sniffed and licked him. Their obvious happiness about being together made Eduardo glad he'd given in to his kids' pleas.

Fiona approached, looking in the same direction and then smiling down at him.

He started to get to his feet, but she waved a hand and sat down beside him. "Sorry you caved?" she asked, a dimple tugging at the corner of her mouth.

He dragged his gaze away from it and shook his head. "Once I saw how excited Sparkles was to see Brownie, I was a goner."

"She gets around well on three legs." She hesitated, then added, "Did you know Sofia is making a connection between Sparkles and your wife?"

"What do you mean?"

"She had cancer and was separated from her child. Sofia told me she thought Sparkles wanted to be with Brownie the way your wife would have wanted to be with her and Diego, if she could."

The words hit him unexpectedly hard, and he couldn't speak.

Fiona seemed to read his emotions. She touched his hand and then shifted into a more comfortable position. "You okay?"

He nodded and swallowed the lump in his throat. *Boys don't cry.* He could remember his father saying it, but it was a lie and one he'd never repeated to Diego.

Still, he didn't want to break down in front of her just because his daughter had compared a hurt mama dog to Elizabeth. He was relieved when she changed the subject. "Sparkles is a sweet dog. If you hadn't adopted her, I might have done it myself. So, I'm *really* glad you did."

"I didn't know I could have shifted the burden onto you." He smiled at her and she smiled back, and they were just two parents sharing the humor and the challenges of raising kids.

It was lighthearted. And then it wasn't.

Fiona's eyes were green with gold flecks, and as he held her gaze, they seemed to darken.

His heart stirred in ways it hadn't since he was courting Elizabeth.

She must have detected the intensity, because she looked away. "I… I shouldn't take on any more responsibility, like another dog, because I need to think about what to do next," she said quickly. "After the dog-walking business failed, I thought I would never start another one, but all of a sudden now, I've been considering it again." She still wasn't looking at him.

"What…" He cleared his throat. "What would you do?"

"I keep looking at that barn back behind us. I'm wondering… Could I buy it and make it into a wedding venue? Barn weddings are so popular now, and I love weddings." She met his eyes, looked away and blushed furiously.

He pushed out a chuckle. "Most women do. Have you researched the business side of it?"

A muscle twitched in the side of her face, the same side where the dimple had been. "Yes, but probably not enough. It's not my strong suit."

"Hey." He leaned a little closer, just to try to make her feel better. "No entrepreneur loves the research side of it, at least nobody I know. You have to do it, but that's not the most important skill."

"You think not?" She looked past him toward the old barn behind her property. "I like the idea of a wedding business because I could manage the hours. Do the prep work when I have time, or when the kids are in bed. Slow it down when things are busy at home. So, it would work with raising the kids. And it's a lot of the skills I *am* good at—organizing parties, decorating, caterers and food."

"And romance?" he asked teasingly, and then he could have kicked himself. What kind of a joker said something like that to a lady?

She didn't take it badly, though; she just snorted out a little laugh. "That, I'm not so good at. But I'm not the one who has to be romantic. I'd leave that to my clients."

"Wise."

She leaned back on her elbows. "I don't have much patience, though. Never been able to pay a whole lot of attention to details. So..." She shook her head. "I really shouldn't be planning another business endeavor."

"It takes time," he said. "When I started doing landscaping on the side, it seemed to take forever to get from two clients to five. I must have given out hundreds of business cards. I put up flyers everywhere. I came close to giving up, cashing in the equipment I'd bought and just taking more overtime at Hinton instead."

"How'd you stick with it?" She actually sounded interested.

He leaned over and plucked a blade of grass, held it up to the sun. "I started to realize a business is like a garden. You can't just put in the seeds and expect to be harvesting tomorrow. There's a growth process. Plants need sun and air and water. And time."

"Yeah." She looked over at her terraced vegetable garden, sat up straight to look again and then jumped up and ran over there. "Hey! Eduardo, c'mere!"

He followed, bemused to see her squatting in the grass in front of the terraces, studying the soil like a little kid. "Look! Something's coming up already!"

He studied the ground. "Yep. That's the lettuce. We planted it, what, nine days ago? And it's been nice and warm."

"I'm so excited!" She laughed up at him, her smile broad, eyes dancing.

"What's that, Mommy?" Poppy ran and banged into Fiona, then crouched to stare at the ground. The two of them looked so cute together, like the cover of a seed catalog.

An impression that was instantly broken when Brownie came loping over and ran carelessly through the garden, taking out a good six inches of lettuce seedlings just on the one pass.

He put his fingers to his lips and gave a loud whistle. Brownie stopped, and Sparkles, who'd been following her son, froze as did all the kids.

"Okay, everyone. I need your help keeping the dogs out of the garden until we get a fence up."

"We need a fence?" Fiona frowned. "I'd rather have it be open."

"We weren't anticipating two active dogs," he said.

"Yeah, that's true, I guess." She studied the ground Brownie had torn up, picked up a tiny broken seedling. "Guess these little babies aren't going to make it."

"A fence will fix it," he reassured her. "It'll keep the critters out, too."

"Okay," she said with instant trust in his judgment. Then Ryan and Maya tugged at her hands and she followed them across the yard, laughing at some story they were telling. Sofia ran over, and Fiona reached out an arm to include his daughter in with her kids.

He watched them in the twilight, in the guise of replanting a couple of seedlings. Couldn't stop himself, not really.

He only wished he could put up a fence around his heart to keep out the uncomfortable feelings he was having toward the very pretty mother who grew more appealing the more time he spent with her.

Chapter Seven

❧

"Are you sure it's okay to leave all four of them with you?" Fiona asked Daisy the next Saturday. Colorful kids' crafts lined the tables in the activity room of the Senior Towers. Fiona's four kids had never been here before, but Maya had already sat down with a couple of other kids, clearly intrigued by their egg-painting project. A woman with short, stylish white hair and a colorful caftan held up an egg and demonstrated how to paint it.

"Absolutely," Daisy said. "We want kids. That's what this is all about. Right, Adele?"

"Right," the caftan-clad woman said, smiling. "Come on over."

Poppy clung to Lauren and Ryan looked from Fiona to the tables, his brow wrinkled.

"Go ahead, guys," Fiona encouraged them, walking over to the tables with Daisy. Her kids followed. Moments later, Adele had them all set up with materials and she was showing them different ways they could color their eggs.

"They'll be fine," Daisy assured Fiona. "A couple of other kids are coming, I think. We'll keep them entertained, and you can help decorate the lobby and cafeteria. They really need some adult volunteers out there."

"Okay, if you're sure." Truthfully, a couple of hours working and talking with adults sounded blissful.

Behind them, a deep chuckle. "Well, well. Look who's here."

Chief Dion. Fiona looked over at Daisy and saw her friend suck in a breath, her face reddening.

Fiona extended a hand in greeting. "Hey, Chief Dion, what are you doing here?" she asked. "Are you going to paint Easter eggs?"

"If I'm needed," he said, then looked at Daisy. "I didn't know you were volunteering today."

"I didn't know *you* were." Daisy crossed her arms over her chest.

Wanting to ease the awkwardness between the two of them, Fiona cast around in her mind for conversation. "I didn't know you liked working with kids. You don't have any, do you?"

Something flashed in the police chief's eyes. "I... No. No, I don't."

Way to muck things up, Fiona. "I'm sorry, that was a rude question." She glanced over at Daisy, who gave her a half smile and a rueful shrug.

Dion patted Fiona's shoulder. "Don't you worry," he said. "There's a reason I keep getting invited. Every year, I say I won't do it—" he held open a large bag to display a fuzzy costume "—and every year, they talk me into it."

Fiona held back a laugh at the idea of the tall manly police chief in a bunny suit. "The kids will love it."

"Yes, they will," Daisy said, her voice unusually flat.

The sound of more kids' voices made them all turn toward the door, where Sofia and Diego were coming in. "Hey," they both said to the adults and then hurried to the table where Fiona's kids were already deep into wax pencils and egg dye.

Fiona looked to the doorway, and sure enough, there was Eduardo still dressed in the Hinton Enterprises polo shirt and work pants. "Sorry we're late," he said and then looked past Daisy and Dion to focus on Fiona. One dark eyebrow lifted a fraction. "Let me guess," he said slowly, "you're here to decorate the cafeteria."

Dion touched Daisy's arm and nodded toward the kids' table. "Want me to help you supervise?"

"That would be…great." Daisy sounded just a little breathless.

Eduardo's eyes narrowed a little as he looked after them.

"There you are!" Nonna D'Angelo came into the room, her eyes sparkling behind thick glasses. "Come on, the cafeteria decorating is getting started and we need some youngsters to climb ladders and lift heavy boxes." Slyly, she reached up and patted Eduardo's biceps. "I think you're almost as strong as my Vito."

"I doubt that." Eduardo smiled down at the much shorter woman. "But I'm a hard worker. Lead on."

Fiona followed, musing about the interactions she'd just witnessed. Daisy and Dion were rumored to be a couple, but they both claimed to be nothing but friends. Something about the sparkle in Nonna D'Angelo's eyes, though, suggested that the matchmaking seniors had been involved in making sure the two volunteered together.

Was there a similar effort going on with Fiona and Eduardo?

In the cafeteria, chairs had been moved aside to allow those using wheelchairs to access the tables. A group of three women and a man in a red flannel shirt worked on what looked like centerpieces, consisting of low narrow baskets with colored grass, small figurines of rabbits and hens, and colorful ribbons. As they worked, they argued loudly.

"An Easter decoration isn't an Easter decoration without candy," the man said. "We oughta put chocolate eggs all through that grass."

"Kirk, you know that half the people here have diabetes, and the kids who are visiting shouldn't be getting all sugared up." The woman who spoke wove ribbon through a basket's rim and held it up for the others to see. "Do it like this, only with all different colors, and tie it in a pretty bow. I can help if you're not on board," she said to the red-shirted man.

"Kids are *supposed* to get sugared up at Easter," he grumbled, but he obediently took a ribbon and cardboard and followed the woman's lead.

"Over here." Nonna bustled over to a tall stepladder and a couple of baskets of crepe paper, with scissors and tape beside the baskets. She beckoned to Fiona and Eduardo. "Could you two be in charge of making streamers?"

"Sure," Eduardo said. "Right?" He looked at Fiona.

"Right." Her sense of being pushed together with Eduardo was increasing. The disconcerting thing was the little jump in her pulse at the thought of working with him. She clenched her teeth, trying to get back to business.

"Eight or ten of them, meeting at the middle and then back to the opposite wall. And maybe some kind of backdrop for the dessert table." Nonna patted Fiona's arm, then Eduardo's. "Take your time."

Fiona picked up a bright pink roll of crepe paper. "Do you want to climb or twist?" she asked Eduardo. Contrary to Nonna's advice to take their time, she wanted to get this over with as soon as possible. She couldn't believe that she was now volunteering with Eduardo, in addition to living on the same property and working on the garden together. Attending the same church. Was there a day of the week when they didn't see each other?

And unfortunately, the more she saw of him, the more she liked him. He'd spoken truthfully—he *was* a hard worker, and she admired that. But he was never too busy to listen to a child's story or clean up the pews after services or help carry a heavy package. He had a ready laugh that drew people to him. His faith didn't just show up on Sundays but was an integral part of his life, as she'd seen in the way he talked to Sofia and Diego, guiding them toward being good Christians and good people.

Not to mention that the man was gorgeous. As he climbed the ladder, reached up to examine the ceiling and then looked down at her, eyes sparkling, she had to restrain herself from simpering like a middle schooler on her first crush.

"So," he said, "if I twist it around these braces, do you think it'll hold? I'm not exactly an expert at crepe paper streamers. In school, it was the girls who decorated for the prom."

"I'd say tape it." She handed him up the crepe paper and the roll of tape. "Did you go? To your prom, I mean?" Then she felt heat rise in her face. Why had she asked that question? Was it any of her business?

"I did," he said. "I took Elizabeth. It was one of our first dates." His hands went still for a moment, and then he smiled down at her. "Good times."

"That's nice. Nice to know high school sweethearts can make it last." She'd been awkward in high school and hadn't had a real boyfriend.

"We were together since age fifteen," he said. "Not that our parents let us date that young, but we ate lunch together at school and held hands in the hallways when we could get away with it." He shook his head as if shaking off the memories. "How about you? Did you go to prom?"

She nodded. "I went. With a boy who was at least a foot shorter than me. I wore flats and tried to hunch down for the photos, and he was practically on tiptoe. We got ourselves closer to the same height for the picture, but the expressions on our faces!" She gave a fake wince. "Totally miserable."

He chuckled. "I had the same problem. I was already six-three in tenth grade, and Elizabeth was a foot shorter. Dancing was a little awkward." He smiled. "But we figured it out."

And they'd been very happy together, from the sound of things.

"Was your husband tall?" he asked. "Not that it's any of my business," he added quickly, attaching the paper on one end and handing the streamer down to her. "Here. You twist, and I'll move the ladder to the center."

"He was about my height," she said, walking backward beside him, twisting the paper. "He didn't like for me to wear heels."

Eduardo laughed. "We men. We get our egos caught up in all the wrong things."

Miss Minnie Falcon approached, pushing her walker. She watched as they attached the next loop of crepe paper to a crossbar in the center of the ceiling.

"Do you think it looks okay?" Fiona asked her.

Miss Minnie waved a wrinkled hand. "It's fine. As long as the residents see some color, they'll be happy, and the same with the children. They'll all be busy playing games and eating candy."

"No candy, Minnie," said the same woman

who'd restricted the man from adding it to the centerpieces.

Miss Minnie waved a hand and turned away. "There'll be candy, don't you worry," she said quietly to Fiona and Eduardo. "Your kids will have a wonderful time. They're coming, aren't they?"

"Our kids are here now," Eduardo said, climbing down from the ladder. "I think they're part of the practice drill for the big party next week. Daisy and Adele are in charge."

"And Dion," Fiona reminded them. "He's dressing up as the Easter bunny later. I would guess he'll at least have a few jelly beans to pass around."

"Sugar-free," said the woman at the table.

"Sugar-free candy gives me gas," said Kirk, the red-shirted man.

Fiona looked at Eduardo. His dark eyes twinkled with the same suppressed laughter that threatened to bubble up inside of her. He jerked his head sideways toward the next corner of the room and she nodded and took the roll of crepe paper from him, twisting it as she backed away from the now-lively altercation between Miss Minnie and the table decorators.

"I'm glad we're just on ceiling duty," he said as soon as they were out of the elders' earshot.

"Wouldn't want to get in the middle of the sugar versus sugar-free debate."

"Me, either." She waited while he set up the ladder and then handed him the roll. "I do my best to keep a balance with my kids, food-wise, but Easter is no-holds-barred candy at my place. Hope that won't be a problem for you, because I'm sure our kids will want to share the wealth."

"Just as long as you don't steal all the peanut butter eggs," he said, pulling his face into a mock-serious expression. "Those are *mine*, lady."

"No way, they're my favorites, too! You won't be seeing any from the Farmingham household."

"Wait a minute." He narrowed his eyes at her. "You're a basket thief, too?"

"Of course!"

"Openly or stealth?"

"Oh, stealth, for sure. But I think Lauren's onto me. She took her basket to her room and hid it in the closet last year."

"You need to perfect your approach."

They were both laughing, gazes locked, standing close together. Something arced between them, a connection of humor and empathy and, maybe, something more.

Maybe if Eduardo were to bend a little closer and kiss her, she wouldn't pull back.

But what was she thinking? Women like Fiona didn't get men like Eduardo.

Not only that, but they were standing at the edge of a retirement center cafeteria, all tile floors and Formica tables, laughter and small talk drifting over from the few groups of people at the tables.

They were still looking at each other. She needed to pull back, and quickly.

"I used to decorate like that for all the school dances," said a shaky voice behind them.

Just in time. Fiona turned and saw a tiny woman in a wheelchair. "Miss Elsie! I haven't seen you in church lately."

"Can't do anything much now." The woman looked down at her own body with what seemed to be disgust.

Eduardo knelt beside her and took her tiny hand. "Hey, Miss Elsie. We could use some help with the decorating if you're up for it."

"I don't know what use I could be. Can't walk since I broke my hip. Don't have much energy."

Eduardo took the crepe paper roll from Fiona and placed it in the older woman's hands. "If you do the twisting while Fiona rolls you along and I get the ladder set up, it'll go a lot faster. Fiona can get on the step stool beside me, and you can hand it up to her. I won't have to keep climbing up and down."

The woman narrowed her eyes at him. "Don't you patronize me, Eduardo Delgado."

"We could use the help, but it's up to you," he said with a shrug and climbed the ladder.

Fiona hurried over to the wall and grabbed the step stool, setting it up between the tall ladder and the wheelchair.

Miss Elsie began twisting the crepe paper, and when it was ready, she handed it to Fiona, who handed it to Eduardo.

It was, in fact, a quicker and easier way to work.

Had Eduardo *wanted* to get the job over with quickly? Did he dislike working alone with Fiona? Or was he just being kind to an old woman who seemed in need of cheering up?

Fiona blew out a breath, and with it, her childish thoughts. What mattered was that the cafeteria began looking more and more festive, and a woman who'd been complaining of uselessness felt useful.

"How much of that crepe paper do you have?" Miss Elsie asked.

"Lots. Why?"

"It looks nice if you twist two together," Miss Elsie said. She took a pink strand, held it together with a white one and demonstrated. "And if you loop the ends around, like so, it covers the tape." As she spoke, she added a couple of twists and folds to the end of the streamer to make a flower effect.

"Wow, that's pretty!" Fiona studied the flower. "Can you show me how?"

"It does look better." Eduardo took the paper flower from Fiona and climbed the ladder to affix it to the spot where the streamer was taped to the ceiling.

"We're obviously rank amateurs," Fiona said. "Do you think we need to redo the ones that are done?"

Elsie waved her hand. "Goodness, no. It's a party for kids and old people. No one needs or wants perfection."

"Well," Eduardo said as he carried the ladder to the next location, Fiona pulling Elsie backward so she could twist the strands, "we're a little bit closer to perfection because of you. Thank you."

Elsie beckoned for Fiona to bend closer as Eduardo climbed the ladder. "He's a charmer, that one," she said. "Hold on to him."

"I'm not…" Fiona broke off. She wasn't *with* Eduardo, and she didn't want anyone to think she was; on the other hand, making a big deal out of how they *weren't* together didn't seem like the right move, either.

She set up her stepladder, took the twisted paper from Elsie and climbed up to Eduardo.

They were taping up the last streamer when a man spoke up behind her. "Where you from, honey?"

Fiona turned on the stepladder and looked down to see Kirk, the red-shirted man who'd complained about candy and gas, pointing at her. "I'm from Illinois," she said.

His bushy grey eyebrows lifted. "They grow 'em tall out there, don't they?"

Heat rose in her face as she descended the stepladder, wanting to get out of the spotlight. Talk about embarrassing! Would her size *always* be the first thing people noticed about her?

"Kirk Whittaker, you shut your mouth." Nonna D'Angelo said. "Fiona just needs a taller man than you are, that's all." She pulled herself to her full height of, at most, five foot three and glared at Mr. Whittaker, who wasn't much bigger.

The old man's face turned as red as his shirt. He glanced around, stiffened his back and squared his shoulders.

As she stood beside the stepladder, her face still warm, a thought struck Fiona: in addition to being about the same height as she was, Reggie had been slender, not muscular like Eduardo.

Maybe that was why he'd always told her to wear low heels and lose weight. Maybe he'd just felt small around her.

Another man, even shorter than Mr. Whittaker and sporting ancient-looking baggy blue jeans, strolled over. "What's that you say about tall women?"

Fiona groaned inwardly.

"Now, me," the jeans-clad man said around the toothpick he was chewing, not waiting for an answer, "I like a tall gal. My Lulu was six foot and did some modeling. I was proud to be at her side, even when she wore those high spike heels."

Miss Minnie Falcon shook her head and looked directly at Fiona but spoke loudly enough for all to hear. "We're God's workmanship, and that's the important thing. And all this focus on appearances takes away from what's truly important. What's in our hearts." She frowned sternly at the two men.

Obviously understanding the reprimand, they looked away from the stern former Sunday school teacher and got very busy cleaning up from the centerpiece-decorating project.

Still up on the ladder, Eduardo cleared his throat. "We'd better finish up," he said and climbed down. The elders, with the exception of Elsie, started carrying supplies to the boxes that lined one side of the room.

Fiona partially turned to find Eduardo standing closer than she'd expected. "I'm with Miss

Minnie," he said in a half whisper. "We're all God's workmanship. And he did a particularly fine job on you."

Heat rose in her face again and she turned toward him. "Eduardo…"

"Inside and out," he added, looking directly into her eyes.

And then he backed up and moved the ladder to the next location, leaving Fiona to push Elsie's wheelchair. Meanwhile, Fiona's heart was pounding like Ryan's snare drum, way too hard and loud. Was it her imagination, or did handsome Eduardo feel something romantic toward her? And if he did…was he likely to do anything about it?

Be careful. Don't get sucked in.

She liked Eduardo and thought him to be a good person, but he was a man. And in her experience, men were genetically predisposed to betray women.

Especially women like her.

Chapter Eight

Eduardo berated himself as he carried a ladder toward the storage room, Fiona walking in front of him.

Why'd you tell her how good she looks? Why would you want to say a thing like that? Why do you keep half hitting on her when you know you can't take it anywhere?

Fiona paused at the window, and the sunlight set her red hair on fire. She glanced back at him, wariness in her eyes. She knew he was interested, all right.

And that was bad. Because no matter how interested he was, he couldn't act on it. He kept walking past her, ignoring her magnetic pull.

"Looks like the kids are outside," she said as he passed.

"Go ahead. I'll be out in a minute." Or more. However long it took to calm his fool self down.

Ten minutes later, he'd put the ladders away, washed his hands and splashed water on his face. At the same time, he gave himself a lecture about how he was committed to his kids, and only his kids, and how he wasn't in the market for a relationship.

Still, when he walked outside to see his children and Fiona's all clustered around a long bench with a giant white Easter bunny, with Fiona watching from across the wide deck, his resolve started to melt away.

Why was it, again, that he couldn't take a stab at forming a family with Fiona?

Poppy sat on the bench off to one side, a good six or eight feet away from the crowd around the bunny. She had a basket in her hands and was rhythmically putting candy into her mouth. Chocolate, if the smears on her hands and face were any indication.

As he approached, Fiona half turned.

"Poppy's okay?" he asked.

Fiona smiled fondly at her youngest child. "She's scared of the Easter Bunny," she said, "but not too scared to take the basket of chocolate eggs he offered her."

"Smart kid." And she was cute, too, with her flyaway blond hair and big serious eyes.

The bunny held out a basket to the other kids, and they all took pieces of paper out of it. The two older girls read theirs and ran off quickly. Maya, Ryan and Diego, slower readers, stood studying theirs.

Diego's forehead wrinkled and the color heightened in his cheeks. All of a sudden, he flung the paper back at the bunny. "This isn't the right way to do an egg hunt," he yelled.

Maya grabbed the fluttering sheet of paper. "If you don't want to find your surprise, I'll take it."

"Gimme that!" Diego grabbed the paper roughly out of Maya's hand.

"Hey!" Ryan said, stepping protectively in front of Maya. "Don't be mean to my sister!"

Instantly, without looking at each other, Fiona and Eduardo both headed toward the kids.

Eduardo reached the small group first and gripped Diego's shoulder firmly. "What's going on? You know better than to talk to people that way."

"I hate this egg hunt," Diego muttered, looking away.

"He was mean to Maya." Ryan glared at Diego.

"Diego, do you need to apologize?" Eduardo asked.

"It's no big deal." Maya shrugged and turned toward the lawn where colorful eggs peeped through the grass. "I'm gonna go hunt for eggs."

"Sorry," Diego grunted after her.

"And I'm gonna find my surprise," Ryan said.

He looked at Fiona and Eduardo and held up his square of paper. "The Easter Bunny made it like a treasure hunt, and every kid gets a special surprise." Then he added in a whisper, "I *think* the Easter Bunny is Police Chief Coleman."

From inside the bunny, a low chuckle sounded. "Oh, no, no, no. Nobody knows the true identity of the Easter Bunny, young man."

Eduardo held out a hand for Diego's paper, then studied its small closely printed letters and immediately understood the problem. He turned to Diego. "Come on, let's sit down and look at your clue sheet together."

"I don't want to do it."

The Easter Bunny had been quiet, but now he stood. "Time for the old EB to go cool off," he said. Leaning toward Fiona, he whispered, "This suit is as hot as wearing a plastic bag in the desert at high noon."

She laughed and touched the bunny's arm. "You poor thing. You're enjoying every minute of this, and you know it."

The bunny chuckled again, and Eduardo felt jealousy knife through his chest.

"I might enjoy it," Dion added, quietly enough that the kids didn't hear, "except it smells like every other sweaty guy that ever rented it." He patted Diego's and Ryan's heads with a giant paw and headed toward the door into the Towers.

Eduardo was glad to see him go, which was ridiculous. Was he seriously jealous of a man in a bunny suit? He squatted in front of his son with the clue sheet. "You know what to do when you start getting frustrated, right?"

"Oh, Dad…" Diego's lower lip stuck out a little, his face still reminiscent of the toddler he'd been.

Eduardo clenched his teeth to keep from reading the page aloud to his son. "You know the steps to take."

"I just want to find my egg! I don't wanna go slow and sound it out."

That made sense. Again, Eduardo fought the urge to just do the work for his son. "Is there another way you could get it done?"

Diego sighed and turned to Ryan. "I'm sorry I was mean to Maya," he said. "You want to look for our eggs together? I have dyslexia, and it's hard for me to read this." He took the clue sheet from his dad and held it up.

"Sure, I'll help," Ryan said. "Let's go!"

And they ran off together.

Fiona stared after them and then sat down on the steps of the deck. Her forehead wrinkled and she cocked her head to one side.

He shouldn't sit down next to her, and there wasn't much room on the step. He'd have to sit close.

Plus, the deck's fences and surrounding bushes gave them privacy. The last thing they needed.

But he was curious about what put that thoughtful expression on her face, so he sat down against his better judgment. "What?" he asked her.

"Diego has dyslexia," she said slowly, "and he does just fine. He takes steps to get help when he needs to."

"He gets embarrassed sometimes," Eduardo said. "But his teachers and I drill into him that it's not his fault. He learns differently, and sometimes he needs a different kind of help." He looked after his son and pride welled in his chest. "He's getting better about dealing with it."

"Eduardo," she said, gently grasping his arm, "do you think I could get help with my math thing, even though I'm an adult? Learn strategies to work around it?"

He tried to ignore the way her touch seemed to radiate through his body. "Of course you could."

"How?"

"Well… I'm no expert, but I do get a magazine from a national organization about learning disabilities. They have a whole section for adults with LD."

"Can I look at it sometime? Soon?"

"Of course. I'll get you a couple of copies tonight. I'm sure there are online resources, too."

"Because, the way Diego acted just then?" She spoke rapidly, her cheeks pink. "That's how I used to feel. Still do, sometimes."

"Like when we were looking at spreadsheets at the Chatterbox?"

She nodded. "Exactly. I've learned to cover it up under a ditzy-female routine, but I'm not laughing on the inside. Except now, I am. Or smiling, at least. Because maybe I can get help with it."

"I'm sure you can." *Why hadn't her parents gotten her help long ago?*

"And maybe," she went on, her eyes glowing, "maybe I can even get to where I can have a business again." Her hand tightened on his arm. "Oh, Eduardo, that would be so fantastic. It's been my dream, ever since I became a mom, to have a part-time business and stay home with the kids. I have dozens of ideas."

She was so pretty that he was tongue-tied. He just nodded like an idiot and kept staring at her.

She let go of his arm, maybe misinterpreting his silence. "I'd better not get too excited about this, right? I mean, who knows whether I'm one of those people who can be helped? I'm a whole lot older than Diego." She slid away from him, as much as possible on the narrow step. "I'm sorry to go so crazy on you, just because I saw your son figure something out."

Seeing her get so excited about the future and about new possibilities had warmed Eduardo's heart. Seeing her back off made it hurt. He didn't want her to retreat into fear and shame again.

He wanted to help her blossom.

Like it had a will of its own, his hand reached out to brush back a strand of hair that had fallen over her cheek. Once there, his thumb decided to stroke her jawline, just a little.

And now, a whole different kind of emotion came into her gold-flecked eyes, in fact, a mixture of them: fear and worry, but also that awareness he'd seen a time or two before.

He drew in a breath and tried to smile reassuringly. "It's nice to see you excited about the future." Which would have worked as an excuse for his touching her, except that his hand was still up there, cupping her face.

Her own hand came up to his. To pull it away? No. Just to rest on top of his. Her breath was a little ragged, too, almost as ragged as Eduardo's own.

He knew he shouldn't kiss her. There were reasons, lots of reasons. It was just that, right now, he couldn't exactly remember what they were.

"We shouldn't…" she began. But her hand clutched his, convulsively, holding it to her face.

"I know." He leaned closer. "Tell me no."

Her eyes were wide. Slowly, she shook her head. "No."

"No, don't kiss you? Or no, you're not going to tell me no?"

"No," she said in a husky whisper, "I'm not going to tell you no."

Fiona felt her heart turn to butter as Eduardo's lips brushed hers, then came back to linger, warm against her mouth. She yielded to him, dizzily, and tightened her hand over his to steady herself. After a moment he pulled away and rubbed his cheek against hers, rough as sandpaper against her softness.

Voices echoed in her mind: *Why would someone like him kiss someone like you? You should be thankful to get any man. Does he mean it, or is it a lie like Reggie's kisses were?*

She pulled back, trying to shake the thoughts out of her head the way you'd shake away a buzzing insect.

Eduardo's warm brown eyes held concern along with caring. "Hey. What's going on in that head of yours?" His tone was deeper than usual.

"Nothing," she said in defiance of the voices. She leaned fractionally closer and Eduardo brushed his lips over hers again.

"Dad!" Sofia's voice was close.

Fiona and Eduardo pulled instantly apart.

"My mommy's kissing your daddy!" Poppy giggled from Sofia's arms.

Fiona's heart pounded as she stood quickly. "We're good friends," she said, uncomfortable with the breathless sound of her voice. She reached out to take Poppy from Sofia.

But Poppy struggled down and ran across the lawn toward the other kids. Her stomach knotting, Fiona hurried after her. But not before she caught a glimpse of Sofia's mistrustful expression and heard her say, "Dad? You're not supposed to kiss anybody but Mom."

Poppy reached the other children. "Our mommy kissed Mr. Delgado!" she crowed, obviously thrilled to be the one with the news for once.

Four heads snapped in her direction. Four pairs of eyes went rounder.

Fiona felt sick inside. What kind of parents were they, to share a stolen kiss practically in full view of their children?

A kiss that couldn't go anywhere, ever?

Eduardo sat in his pickup truck in the parking lot of the Senior Towers, trying to do damage control with his kids.

What had possessed him to kiss Fiona? And to do it there, where any of their kids could come around the corner and see them…as Sofia and Poppy in fact had done? How selfish they'd been to risk hurting innocent young children whose hearts had already been broken once before.

Fiona walked by on the way to her SUV, her kids surrounding her like a brood of chicks with a mother hen. They were all talking excitedly, but Fiona's face was drawn tight.

They glanced at each other, but all he could see in her eyes was regret.

"Why *did* you kiss Mrs. Farmingham, Dad?" Diego sounded confused, like he was trying to work out a new math problem in his head.

"Because he *likes* her, dummy." Sofia's arms were crossed over her chest.

Eduardo shot up a prayer for guidance. How did you protect young minds and hearts while being honest with them about life?

"I kissed her because…" Eduardo sought for the truth. "Because I like her very much."

"We like her, too, Dad," Sofia said in the snarky voice she hadn't been using as often lately. "But we don't hide behind bushes *kissing* her."

"Does it mean you're going to get married?" Diego asked.

Eduardo blew out a sigh and shook his head. "No. I've told you before, I don't have any plans to get married again. You two are my focus."

"And Mom was your wife," Sofia said.

"But Mom's gone," Diego pointed out, "and maybe Daddy wants another wife now."

Eduardo hated the way that sounded. "You kids know how much I loved your mother," he said through a tight throat. "How much I miss her. I wish she could be here with us right now."

"But she can't," Sofia said flatly, "so you're kissing Mrs. Farmingham now."

"That…that was a onetime thing," he told them. "I don't think we'll be kissing each other again." Not with the expression he'd seen on Fiona's face.

But, oh, that moment had been sweet. He'd felt like a bear coming out of hibernation after a long, long winter. Coming alive again in the spring. Waking up to a new world.

He wasn't a good choice for any woman, he reminded himself. He'd made a commitment to his kids, no one else.

"Mr. Hinton was married before and his wife died," Diego pointed out. "And then he married Mrs. Hinton, and now Mindy has a mom again. And a little brother." Diego sounded a little wistful.

"That's true," Eduardo admitted.

But Sam Hinton also had a stellar record of taking care of his first wife. She'd lived in luxury throughout her cancer treatments, with visits to specialists around the world.

And it still didn't save her, a voice inside reminded him.

"It would be weird having the Farmingham kids as brothers and sisters." Sofia sounded slightly intrigued by the possibility. "I'd have a sister my exact age, like a twin."

"Look, guys," Eduardo said, "let's stop talking about that like it's going to happen. Let's stop at…" He cast about for something that might distract them. "Let's stop at Taco Nation and pick up dinner and watch movies all night."

"All *night*?" Diego said.

At the same time, Sofia said, "Taco *Nation*?"

"All night until bedtime, and yes. Just this once."

"We haven't gone to Taco Nation since the night after Mom died," Sofia said.

Eduardo let his head sink back against the headrest. He'd forgotten about that miserable last-minute trip. Would hitting the fast-food Mexican place bring back bad memories for all of them?

He wanted to stop thinking. To stop making mistakes. "Buckle up," he said and started to pull out of the Senior Towers parking lot.

But the sound of sirens made him hit the brakes. An ambulance squealed into the parking lot and headed to the front door of the Towers. The sirens clicked off and the paramedics rushed inside.

He, Sofia and Diego sat watching. Nobody told Eduardo to hurry up. Nobody spoke.

Were they all three remembering the ambulance that had come for Elizabeth multiple times? Until the last time when there'd been no more need for speed?

He didn't want to stick around the Senior Towers watching to see who the patient was. Which friend. Whether the ambulance would fly off with lights and sounds or drive at a slow, sedate pace into the night.

He didn't want his kids to see it, either.

Swallowing hard, he put the truck into gear. "Taco Nation, here we come," he said, wondering whether his voice sounded as fake to his kids as it did to him.

"I'm not actually that hungry," Sofia said.

"Me, either," Diego said. "Where's my handheld?"

Eduardo felt around for the small gaming device and handed it back to Diego. Without her even having to ask, he handed his phone to Sofia so she could play her games on it. And he drove home slowly. For a day that had started out so promising, he definitely felt beat-up now.

After finally getting her overexcited kids into bed, Fiona collapsed back onto the couch at her house.

She lay there, flicking channels on the television; but when she finally recognized that she couldn't distract herself from her thoughts, she clicked the power off.

He'd kissed her. Eduardo had kissed her.

He'd kissed *her*. The woman who had to shop at the tall women's clothing store in Cleveland. Who'd repeated third grade and barely passed the math competency test required for high school graduation. Whose business had failed and whose husband had betrayed her.

We are God's workmanship, Miss Minnie had said.

Eduardo had said… What was it? *He did a particularly fine job on you.*

And then he'd kissed her. Her fingers rose to touch her lips as she remembered.

Maybe, just maybe, there was something new and wonderful in her future.

She thought of Diego and his frustration and grabbed her phone to look up *adult learning disabilities*. She was reading about something called "dyscalculia," with a sense of amazed recognition, when a text came in.

Kids in bed? Meet out by the garden?

Eduardo wanted to see her! She hugged herself and rushed into the bathroom to comb her hair. She checked the bedrooms and found all four kids sleeping soundly. Only then did she text back.

For a little bit, can't stay.

Should she put on a different shirt? No, that would seem like she was trying too hard. But definitely a little perfume. And she should brush her teeth. Just in case.

She forced herself to walk at a slow pace toward the garden. In the moonlight, there was Eduardo—tall muscular Eduardo.

A sense of hope and possibility made her heart knock around wildly in her chest.

He didn't walk to meet her but stood beside the fence post he'd just pounded into the ground yesterday. His face was somber.

Something was wrong.

She stopped a full four feet away from him and cocked her head, studying his face.

No, this didn't seem like a kissing-type encounter after all.

"Are you okay?" he asked. "Are your kids okay?"

She nodded, a couple quick jerks of her head up and down. "Yeah. We're fine. Um, you and yours?"

He shook his head. "Lots of questions."

"From you, or from them?"

"Both." He looked up at the starry sky as if seeking guidance and then looked at her straight on and met her eyes. "Look, Fiona…"

She lifted a hand to stop his speaking. She didn't want to hear it. Not from Eduardo.

"I know," she said rapidly. "I know, it's not… It was nothing. It's not going anywhere."

"It wasn't nothing," he said, "but you're right. It can't."

"Is…is that what you wanted to tell me?" Her voice sounded a little shrill. "Because I knew that, Eduardo. What did you think, that I'd take it all seriously? That I'd expect a marriage proposal because we shared a little kiss?"

Who *was* this woman talking so lightly about the most amazing kiss of her life?

"My kids asked if we were going to get married," he said, his voice serious.

"Oh, mine did, too." They'd bugged her about it, actually. They *wanted* her to marry Eduardo, wanted Sofia and Diego to be a part of the family. They were already talking about how they'd rearrange their bedrooms to fit them in.

Now she pushed out a laugh. "Kids. No sense of perspective."

"Right." Eduardo looked off to the side. "I just wanted to make sure, to see if you... Well, to see if you were okay. That was pretty intense for a minute there."

She waved a hand. "I'm fine. Fine! We're friends who got a little carried away, that's all. It wouldn't work between us, anyway. I'm sorry you wasted a minute worrying about it."

Her mouth continued to talk. She was fine. They were all fine. They'd reassure their kids that they were just friends. No upsets, no changes, nothing to worry about.

Her heart curled up in a tiny little ball in her chest, weeping.

"Okay, Fiona," Eduardo said finally. "That's all good, then. I should get back to the kids."

"Me, too," she said quickly. "I should get back to my kids, too."

"Good night, then." He gestured toward her house. "Go on. I'll watch until you get inside."

"It's Rescue River." She forced a cheerful smile. "I'm totally safe."

"I'll watch," he said gently. "See you safe inside."

"Okay. Good night." She turned and nearly ran toward the door of her house, eyes blurring.

Because she was anything but safe inside. Not when Eduardo had shoved her away, just as she'd known, in her heart, that he would.

Chapter Nine

When Eduardo pulled his truck into the parking lot by the pond the next morning, he wasn't surprised to see Fiona and her kids pulling gear from her SUV.

Of course they were coming to today's fishing derby. Everyone in town was here.

In fact, he was late. As the person supervising the fishing of the eight-to ten-year-olds, he should have arrived half an hour early. But getting out of bed had proved to be a chore.

He'd tossed and turned most of the night, his mind cycling restlessly through particular moments. Sofia's accusation: *you're not supposed to kiss anyone but Mom.* Little Poppy's glee as she ran off to tell the other kids—and anyone else in earshot, presumably—about the romantic moment she'd seen. Fiona's stricken face last night in the garden before she'd brushed off his remarks with a carelessness that had surprised him.

And most of all, the bittersweet rightness of holding Fiona in his arms.

"There's Lauren and Ryan," Diego said. "Let's go with them."

He was opening his mouth to respond when he saw Fiona tug her eldest two back toward her and walk in the opposite direction from where he stood with his kids.

He dawdled at his truck until the Farminghams were out of sight and then headed toward the pond, where organized chaos reigned.

On one side was a large wading pool set up with toy fishing lines. A sign read *Two-to Three-year-olds*. Rowdy toddlers darted around while parents tried to keep them from plunging into the pool.

Many residents of the town, those who had grandkids or kids here and those who didn't, had set up lawn chairs. He walked by Mr. Love and Miss Minnie among some other residents of the Senior Towers. Kirk, the man who'd been complaining about sweets and gas yesterday, was at it again, saying, "You mark my words, there's a storm coming. I always feel it in my left knee."

"You and your left knee," muttered Nonna D'Angelo as her grandson, Vito, helped her into her seat.

On a small podium, Lou Ann was setting up chairs and a stand for first-place, second-place and third-place winners. Two older gentlemen stood arguing, one overdressed for the occasion and one underdressed. Mr. Hinton, Senior, and old Gramps Camden had been rivals for Lou Ann's affections for many years. As usual, she was ignoring their blustering and getting things done.

Farther down the shoreline, little Mercedes Camden held a group of kids rapt. As Eduardo and his kids got closer, he saw that Fiona's brood had stopped to listen. "When I was little, I got lost here," Mercedes was saying proudly. "It was winter, and it was cold! I hid under this boat, right here."

"Didn't you freeze?" a girl asked.

"How'd you get found?" That was Ryan, sounding worried.

"My daddy found me," Mercedes said proudly. "And he carried me back to Mama Fern, and now we all live together."

"C'mon, Dad!" Diego was tugging at his arm. "They're about to tell the rules!"

Sure enough, there was a megaphoned explanation of the age groups and prizes for most fish and biggest fish. "We have buckets for everyone, so fill yours with water and keep your fish in it until one of the officials can come measure them. They're the ones in the red hats."

Eduardo looked around to see Vito and Lacey D'Angelo, Buck Armstrong and Troy Hinton all wearing red hats and waving.

After more discussion of safety rules and bait, the officials directed the kids to their places, starting with the youngest and organized by age group.

"The only thing I don't like about fishing," Diego said as they waited their turn, "is killing things."

"It's catch and release, buddy," Eduardo explained. "The fish don't die."

"But the worms do."

"You're weird," Sofia scoffed. "Come on, let's get our buckets!"

The next hour was a blur of helping all the eight-to ten-year-olds bait fishhooks, attach bobbers and throw lines into the water. Amid much tangling and arguing, there was thankfully only one volatile moment when Vito D'Angelo's son, Charlie, landed a hook in the newly curled hair of Paula Camden, the little girl Fern and Carlo Camden had adopted a couple of years ago—a crisis quickly averted by some expert parental intervention. Little Mindy Hinton was the first to catch a fish, and no one begrudged her the honor. Reeling it in had been a challenge with her prosthetic arm, but she'd insisted on doing it herself and she'd succeeded.

Parents watched and helped, and Vito and Lacey stood nearby to measure the fish. The kids laughed and yelled, trying their best to win. The day had gone slightly overcast, perfect for fishing.

But Eduardo didn't feel good. Didn't feel right. Didn't like the distance between him and Fiona, even though he knew that he'd done the right thing, and the only thing he could.

It must have shown, too, because Dion came over and slapped him on the back, then nodded sideways, urging Eduardo away from the group. "Gotta talk to you, man," he said. "They've got it under control. Right?" With a stern look, he recruited two fathers who'd been standing idly by to go over and help the eight-to ten-year-olds.

In an area sheltered from the increasing wind and from prying eyes, Dion glared at Eduardo. "What did you do to Fiona?"

Guilt beat at Eduardo, but he got in front of it with his annoyance at the man's tone. "Not your business what goes on between me and her."

"She's usually a happy person, but she's moping. Not saying a word, even though she's doing concessions with her two best friends."

"Did Daisy send you over here to ask me?" Eduardo demanded.

Dion opened his mouth, closed it and looked to the side. Maybe he was trying to fight a smile. "She and Susan, yeah. But it's true Fiona's upset. Even a lunk like me can see it." He studied Eduardo. "Come to think of it, you're not looking so good yourself. Those bags under your eyes make you look older than me."

Eduardo didn't answer, just turned to walk along the wide woodland trail, and Dion fell into step beside him.

Birds sang overhead and the smell of damp earth rose from the forest floor. For a few minutes, they just walked through the trees, and Eduardo felt a small dose of peace seep into his troubled heart.

"I kissed her," he said finally.

Dion looked over, lifted an eyebrow. "That usually makes people happy, not miserable."

"It did, until our kids caught us."

Dion made a sound suspiciously like a laugh.

Eduardo could see how it could be funny on a sitcom, but in real life, it was more complicated. "Sofia's upset."

"Because…"

"I'm not supposed to kiss anyone but Mom."

"Oh." Dion nodded thoughtfully. "She's not used to it because you've never dated much. How about Diego?"

Eduardo shook his head. "He's more thinking about how it'll be when Fiona and I get married."

"Boy moves fast." Dion clapped Eduardo on the back. "I'm sure they'll get accustomed to the idea soon enough. And kids aren't likely to be traumatized by a kiss. How'd Fiona's kids react?"

He wondered the same thing. "I don't know."

Dion stopped, turned to him. "You don't *know*? What did she say about it?"

"We didn't talk. Not really. I… I felt like that was best."

Dion turned to start walking again. "If you didn't have the sense to… Come on, help me understand it. You kissed her but didn't talk to her afterward? What's going on?"

"I'm a working-class landscaper who let down his first wife when she needed me. Fiona's got a million more appropriate opportunities."

"What if she likes *you*, though?"

"It's a mistake she'll get over soon enough."

Dion shook his head. "You're a bigger fool than I thought. Don't you know who you are in Christ?"

Eduardo stared at him. "What does Christ have to do with it?"

"You're kidding, right?"

"Well, sure, I know Christ has to do with everything, but specifically?" He shrugged. "I don't know how He plays into my love life. Or lack thereof."

Dion threw his hands in the air. "I'm dragging you back to Bible study next week. But seriously. If you made mistakes in your past relationship, you're forgiven. And as for money?" He shrugged. "Just not important. Not to a Christian. Not to Fiona, I'm guessing."

"Come on."

"I mean, sure. You've got to pay your way. No slackers in the Kingdom. But anything beyond that doesn't matter."

"When she could afford to take me on twenty luxury vacations for every camping trip I can offer her?" Eduardo shook his head. "Uh-uh. I'm too old-fashioned for that."

"Maybe she likes camping," Dion said mildly as they came out of the woods. "Ever think of that, my man?"

In front of them, the pond was still lively with groups of kids, families and community people. Golden sun slanted through the darkening clouds. Hard to know if it was going to rain or be warm and sunny.

"I'd better get back to my kids," Eduardo said. "Thanks for the talk."

"Anytime. Think about that Bible study."

"I will." Eduardo started to walk away and

then turned back. "You listening to your own advice about women?"

A half smile creased Dion's dark face. "Touché," he said. "Get to work."

Fiona served up two more hot dogs from the concession stand and was about to turn away when she saw Sofia approaching, her forehead wrinkled.

She leaned out and smiled at the sweet child. No matter what differences Fiona and Eduardo had, the kids were innocent. "What's wrong, honey?"

Sofia held out the front of her white T-shirt to display a bright red spot. "I got ketchup on my favorite shirt, and Daddy said it's going to make a stain."

"Let's see." Fiona came outside the concession stand and knelt to study the stain. "He's right, although if we worked on it fast…"

Sofia's face lit up. "Can we? Please? Daddy's not good with stains."

How many men were? "Come on inside," she said, "and put on one of the derby T-shirts. I'll see what I can do."

Sofia changed in a corner, and Fiona went to work on the stain while Daisy and Susan handled the counter, fetching chips and drinks. A couple of minutes later, Sofia came up beside Fiona. "Is it going to come out?"

"I think so," Fiona said. "See, you rinse it from the back with cold water. That keeps it from setting. And then we rub in some dish soap, like this. And then—" she looked around and located a clean bucket "—we'll let it soak in cool water for a while. I'm pretty sure we got it just in time."

Sofia hugged her. "Thank you sooo much," she said, letting her head rest against Fiona's side for an extra moment.

Fiona wiped her soapy hands and hugged the little girl close. "Sure, honey," she said, her throat tightening.

Like all little girls, Sofia needed a mother's love. A mother's guidance as she grew toward womanhood and started to face a woman's issues.

But Fiona couldn't let herself get too attached to the child. Or the reverse. Especially the reverse. It would be a disaster if Eduardo's kids got attached to her. "Go on out, catch some more fish," she urged. "Look, there's Lauren, and she wants to show you something, it looks like."

As Sofia ran down toward the pond, Dion came back to the grill and immediately he and Daisy started bickering. Susan was fretting because her husband had insisted on taking charge of Sam Junior, who, at four months, hadn't spent a lot of time away from his mama's side.

As for Fiona, after a sleepless night, she wanted nothing more than to go home, plunk the kids in front of some engrossing movie and block out the previous evening.

She'd been so happy, so sure that something wonderful was going to happen with Eduardo. His kiss had been tender and strong, everything a first kiss should be. And despite the semi-disaster of their kids discovering them, she hadn't been too worried. Her kids liked Eduardo and his kids, and the idea of the two families getting closer and spending more time together made them happy.

It had made Fiona happy, too.

But his kind, sober rejection in the garden had swept the rug out from under her, restored her idea of her own romantic future to the same unhappy condition she'd always known it was.

Dion brought in a plate of burgers. "Voilà, ladies! Perfection from the grill."

Daisy leaned over to study them. "Are you sure they're done?"

"Of course I'm sure. I've been grilling since you were in primary school!"

Daisy lifted her hands, palms up. "I was just asking! Why do you always have to bring it back to the age difference?"

Susan lifted an eyebrow at Fiona as she took the burgers from Dion and nodded toward the lake. "Thanks, Dion," she said. "This might be enough for the rest of the day. People are starting to pack up and go home."

"I may just do the same." Dion eyed Daisy. "It's feeling kind of cold in here."

"Fine." Daisy started wiping up the counter with unnecessary vigor. "Do what you want."

"Ladies." Dion gave a mock-salute to the three of them, spun on his heel and walked out of the concession stand, his back straight.

Daisy watched him go, her mouth twisted to one side. Fiona put an arm around her friend.

Eight-year-old Mindy came running in and tugged Susan's arm. "Mama, listen!"

Susan bent down, and Mindy whispered into her ear.

Susan's eyebrows lifted almost into her dark hair. "Is that so?"

"That's what Ryan and Lauren and Sofia and Diego said!"

Susan looked over at Fiona.

Fiona's heart sank. "What's wrong?"

Susan knelt in front of Mindy. "I want you to go on back outside, but don't talk about other people's business again. That's called gossip, and we don't do it."

Mindy stole a glance toward Fiona, looking stricken. "I'm sorry, Mama."

"Run and show Daddy the picture of you and your fish. I know he'll want to get copies for all the relatives."

"Yeah!" Mindy dashed out.

The moment she was gone, Susan grabbed a sign that said *Be Right Back!* and closed the front of the concession stand. Then she turned to Fiona. "You *kissed* him?"

"What?" Daisy squeaked. "Who? Eduardo?"

"Of course Eduardo," Susan said. "And in front of the kids, apparently."

"That part was a mistake," Fiona said as anxiety squeezed at her stomach. "But I'm sure the whole town knows about it by now."

Daisy opened a couple of folding chairs in the darkened end of the concession stand and gently pushed Fiona into one of them. "Sit."

Susan perched on the counter. "Tell us everything."

So, Fiona did. When she'd said it all, even the humiliating rejection in the garden last night, she found herself grim and dry-eyed. "So, it was nothing to him. He's so horribly *kind*, and he wanted to let me down easy. Keep me from making a fool of myself. Which would be fine if my kids weren't set on telling the whole town we're getting married."

"Zero to one hundred, that's kids," Susan said, frowning.

"That conversation in the garden was weird." Daisy reached out to squeeze Fiona's arm. "I'm sorry, hon, I can tell you're upset. But think about it. Could he really have meant it as bad as it sounded?"

"Judging from the way he's avoided me today, yes." Tears pushed at the back of her eyes and a couple escaped, which was ridiculous. Angry at herself, she brushed them away.

Susan grabbed a napkin and handed it to her, just as wind gusted through the half-open window of the booth, blowing over the cardboard stand that held candy and bags of chips.

A father and daughter peeked inside. "Any burgers left?" the man asked.

Susan threw a couple together in record time and shoved them toward the customers. "Donate what you want. Condiments over there." And she hurried back down to the spot where Daisy and Fiona were sitting. "What are you going to do?"

Fiona blotted at her eyes. "What *can* I do? He's made his decision, apparently."

Daisy scooted closer to put an arm around

her. "I'm so sorry, honey. How do you feel about Eduardo?"

"How was it, kissing him?" Susan asked, waggling her eyebrows.

"Stop it!" Daisy scolded. "This is serious."

Fiona blew her nose and waved a hand, half laughing. "It's fine. To answer your question first," she added to Susan, "it was…fabulous, sadly."

"Sad because…" Daisy prompted.

"Because I was starting to like him, and kissing him made me like him even more. And so—" She raised a hand to keep Susan from interrupting. "So it's good he stopped me in my tracks. I should have known a guy like Eduardo wouldn't go for someone like me. I *did* know that, but I… I kind of forgot."

Susan and Daisy glanced at each other. "What do you mean 'someone like you'?" Susan asked.

Fiona gestured at herself. "Tall. Carrying extra weight. Not the sharpest…" She cut off the words, frowning. Maybe it wasn't that she was stupid, as she'd always thought. The moment of insight she'd had watching Diego and the things she'd read last night online came back to her mind for the first time since the miserable talk in the garden.

She was going to pursue that, she vowed to herself. She was going to find out if she had a learning disability and see if she could get help. And *that* was one good outcome of the whole Eduardo fiasco.

"You're totally insane, thinking that you aren't attractive," Daisy was saying. "Do you know what most of us would give to have your height and your looks?"

"Oh, well—" Fiona waved a hand. Women always said things like that. Women looked at the world differently than men did, looked for different things in people.

She was going to stick to women friends and not venture into the world of romantic love again.

"I'm not even going to dignify the whole extra-weight thing with a response," Susan said hotly. "I've *told* you and *told* you about our culture's crazy fixation on women being ultra slim, how it impacts us and hurts our self-esteem. You have three daughters, woman! You've got to stop!"

"You're right. I'll try." Fiona drew in a deep breath and reached out a hand to each of her friends. "You guys are the best. I don't know what I'd do without—"

But her words were cut off by the loudest clap of thunder she'd ever heard. There was a simultaneous flash of lightning, and then rain drummed sudden and hard against the concession stand's metal roof.

"My kids!" Fiona jumped up and ran to the window, peering out through the wall of pelting rain.

"Go, find them." Susan was texting and didn't look up from her phone. "I'm sure Sam has Sammy Junior. We'll clean up here. Go!"

"Bring that shirt from the bucket, would you?" Fiona ran out of the concession stand and was instantly soaked.

Eduardo shepherded the last of six soaking wet kids into the cab of his pickup and scanned the nearly empty parking lot. He'd been mildly worried as the skies had darkened and people had started to pack up and leave, but now... Where was Fiona?

"That came out of nowhere!" One of the remaining dads was throwing buckets and fishing tackle into the back of his truck. "So much for the awards ceremony."

"I wanted to get my award!" Diego's mouth compressed into a thin line. "I earned it and I want it."

Eduardo gave him a warning look. "The awards will be figured out later. Right now, we need to focus on staying safe and getting dry and finding Fiona."

"I hope she has my shirt," Sofia said. "She's good at fixing stains."

"It's more important that she's okay," Lauren said from the crowded back seat.

"Yeah!" Ryan added. Then Poppy started to cry.

"I need for all of you to be very mature." Eduardo got in the driver's seat and wiped a hand across his wet face. "I'm going to pull over to your car. Maybe she's inside." Although, she wouldn't be. She'd be looking for her kids rather than trying to keep herself dry.

"There's Mom!" Ryan shouted.

Eduardo screeched to a halt beside Fiona's SUV. "Where?" But even as he asked, he saw her, or a flash of her. Running, but down toward the pond rather than toward the nearly empty parking lot. And then he lost sight of her in the dark downpour.

"I'm gonna go get her," Ryan said.

"Me, too." Lauren reached for the door handle.

"No." He turned in the front seat to make eye contact with all the children. "You need to stay here. Lauren and Sofia—" he eyeballed the two older girls "—you're in charge. You make sure everyone stays inside the truck. Sing songs or something. Got it?"

They both nodded, eyes wide.

"Is our mommy going to die like our daddy did?" Maya asked.

Poppy started crying louder.

"No way," Eduardo said. "She'll be fine." He jumped out and slammed the door, then started running toward the spot he'd last seen Fiona. Rain pelted his head and shoulders and ran into his eyes.

Fiona *would* be fine. She was probably just looking for the kids. They'd have a good laugh about how wet they'd all gotten.

"Eduardo!"

He blinked and saw someone running in his direction. Two people. Susan and Daisy.

He pressed the keys into Daisy's hands. "Can you watch the kids? They're in my truck. I'm looking for Fiona."

"Will do." She ran in the direction of his truck.

"Did you see Sam and my kids?" Susan sounded half-hysterical.

His impulse to help a woman in distress conflicted with his desire to find Fiona. He hesitated, automatically putting an arm around Susan's shoulders, and squinted around the parking lot. The rain stung his eyes.

A pair of headlights cut through the rain. There was a flash of red. Sam Hinton's Lexus?

"That's our car! I have to—"

"Go." He pushed her lightly toward the car that held her family. And then he turned toward the pond. "Fiona! Fiona, I have the kids!"

No answer. Where *was* she? He ran, his heart

pounding, eyes scanning to the right and the left. His feet splashed in instant puddles and he nearly lost his balance. Had she fallen, too? "Fiona!"

Why had she been running toward the pond?

He zigzagged down that way, searching. And then a flash of lightning illuminated the area.

He saw Fiona lifting the rowboat the kids had clustered around earlier, the one Mercedes had said she'd hidden under when she'd gotten lost.

How was she strong enough to lift it by herself? She was going to hurt her back. He sped up. "Fiona!"

A sickening pop, a flash and a large tree exploded into flying limbs and branches. Lightning!

He didn't see Fiona anymore. Had she been struck?

He ran faster than he'd ever ran in his life, arms and legs pumping, water and mud splashing up into his face.

Steam rose from the tree, but all Eduardo could think of was how hard and fast those branches had flown—like a bomb. "Fiona!"

He got to the spot where the rowboat lay half in the pond. Debris from the lightning-struck tree covered the surrounding mud.

His heart thudding, he lifted the boat. She

wasn't under it. He ran along the shore to the right but didn't see her.

Ran to the left. Looked at the now-murky water and felt a moment's pure terror.

The thought of her four kids losing another parent warred with his own fear. He shoved it all away. *Focus. Find her.*

He spun and ran in the other direction, past the rowboat, scanning both the shoreline and the water now. "Fiona!"

He almost tripped over a large branch but caught himself. Saw a slim white hand.

And then he was lifting the giant tree branch off the pale, still form of Fiona Farmingham.

Chapter Ten

Fiona woke to a jolting, dizzying world with someone holding her impossibly foggy head. Rain, a crash and then awful pain surged in her memory, and she struggled to sit up. "Kids," she rasped, opening her eyes and trying to focus.

"They're fine," said a woman's voice. "They're safe."

"Daisy?" She looked up at her friend's blurry face. Why was Daisy here?

Where *was* here?

"Shh. Lie still." Daisy glanced at someone off to the side. "Go straight to the emergency room. They're waiting for us."

Emergency room? But Fiona couldn't go to the emergency room. She had four kids to care for. Again, she tried to sit up, but a sharp pounding pain in her head made her collapse back down, gasping for air.

There was a screech and jolt, the too-loud bang of a door opening, voices.

"Lightning—"

"Tree branch—"

"Lost consciousness—"

"Head injury—"

Somehow, she was lying down flat, zooming along surrounded by people in scrubs. Clenching her teeth against the nausea, she looked around for someone familiar. "My kids..."

"Your kids are fine," came Daisy's soothing voice. "Safe and dry. Your friends are taking care of them."

But they needed *her*. Especially Poppy. She forced herself up onto her elbows, but pain knifed through her forehead and she collapsed back down again.

More shouts and then the stretcher stopped in a cubicle with beeping machines and too-bright lights and a whole crowd of people.

Daisy's face came into view, directly above Fiona's own. "Do. Not. Worry." Her reassuring smile didn't reach her eyes. "You hear? We're all taking care of your kids and they're fine. And you'll be fine, too." She glanced to the right where a masked doctor was doing something to Fiona's arm. "Right?"

"We'll do everything we can to take care of her. Are you a relative?"

"Her sister."

Fiona blinked at the skill with which Daisy told the lie, but it reassured her, too. Daisy would take care of things. Her kids were okay.

She started to sink back into fog again. If only they'd stop poking and prodding her.

Where was Eduardo? She wanted him. But there was some reason—she couldn't think of it now—why she didn't get to have him.

And suddenly, overwhelmingly, she needed to sleep.

Eduardo sat in the ER waiting room, elbows on knees, hands clasped tight. The disinfectant-heavy hospital smell made him queasy, and a heaviness in his chest weighted him down. In his experience, hospital visits didn't end well.

Around the waiting room, a few family clusters sat, talking and looking at their phones. A television, sound off, showed talking heads. A low, well-modulated voice sounded from the hospital intercom: "Smythe family? Smythe family to the reception desk, please." A teenage boy went to the drinking fountain with a uniformed police officer a few feet behind him.

Everyone here had a story, but Eduardo couldn't rouse any curiosity about anyone's but Fiona's.

If he hadn't been having a stupid fight with

her, she wouldn't have gone running off alone to find her kids. They'd have been in good communication, and when that sudden rain came up, they'd have gotten their kids into their respective vehicles and driven home like every other family at the fishing derby.

He'd have texted her to let her know he had her kids in his truck.

Why hadn't he taken the time to text her?

If he had, they'd be safe and dry inside one of their homes right now.

Instead, the kids were terrified, back at Fiona's house with Sam, Susan and Lou Ann. Of course, they didn't believe the adults' assurances that everything would be okay. All of them knew, way too young, that things didn't always turn out okay, no matter what the grown-ups said.

He should have protected them from this new worry, but he hadn't.

To his own surprise, he was including Fiona's kids in his slate of mishandled responsibilities. Since when had he started thinking of them as his own?

When you fell in love with Fiona, you idiot.

That thought stopped him. He wasn't really in love with Fiona. Was he?

He blew out a sigh as his heart twisted and turned. Yeah. In that moment when he'd lifted the branch off her lifeless-looking body, he'd realized it for certain: he was in love with her. Which was a disaster for him, personally, and was potentially a disaster for her.

The double doors to the back of the ER opened and Daisy came out. Instantly, he was on his feet and walking toward her, his heart pounding, trying to read her expression. "How is she?"

"She'd be better if you hadn't made her feel bad about herself yesterday," Daisy snapped. She sank into a chair.

Yesterday. Yesterday had started with a wonderful time decorating the cafeteria at the Senior Towers, and then there'd been that unwise but very delightful kiss. But next had come the kids and the guilt and the memory that he shouldn't be starting up a relationship with her at all. He'd been trying to ease her away from him, disentangle them so she wouldn't be hurt.

Not knowing what else to do, he sat down beside Daisy.

She glared at him. "If you hadn't been fighting, Susan and I wouldn't have had her holed up in the back of the concession stand with the window shut. This would never have happened!"

Guilt washed over him, a crashing wave. It wasn't anything he hadn't already told himself, but hearing it from Daisy—

He let his head sink into his hands. Familiar remorse pressed him down. He should never have moved into the carriage house, should have known that something would go wrong. The bleakness was an echo and a reminder of how he'd failed Elizabeth.

He turned his head sideways to face Daisy. "I know. I take responsibility. But is she going to be okay?"

She bit her lip, gripped his arm, shook it. "I'm sorry, Eduardo. Cancel everything I just said."

"No, you're right. If I'd only let her know I had her kids—"

"It's not your fault. I should never have said that," Daisy interrupted. "Or if it is, I'm just as much to blame. I'm feeling guilty because I kept her inside the concession stand instead of paying attention to how that storm was kicking up."

"You were trying to help."

"Sure, I was. But it was about me, too, because I wanted to talk about female self-esteem and I was having trouble with Dion, and…" Her voice started to crack. "And she has those four kids, those poor kids…"

"Wait." Eduardo's heart beat much too fast and he knelt in front of her. "Daisy. Is she going to be okay? What do the doctors say?"

"I don't know," she choked out. "They're acting weird. Or I think they are. I don't know." She paused. "They're asking her all kinds of questions about stuff like dates and math problems and current events. They're testing her reflexes. And they said they want her to have…" Her voice broke and she took a deep breath. "A CT scan. They want to do a CT scan."

That didn't sound good.

He grabbed a tissue box from an end table and handed it to Daisy. "Do you think they'll let me in? I saw what happened. Maybe there's information I could give…"

Daisy wiped her eyes and shook her head. "I said I was her sister, but it's only a matter of time until they find out I'm not even a relative. I guess we should call her mom, but that'll be more of a problem than a help, from what I understand of their relationship, so I'm holding off. But I know they'll ask for next of kin…"

Eduardo's heart was a giant heavy stone.

"Attention," said the intercom. "Would the party accompanying patient Fiona Farmingham please come to the desk?"

Daisy stood and hurried toward the reception desk. Eduardo followed her.

"You're Fiona's sister?" asked a doctor in scrubs, standing behind the receptionist.

Daisy hesitated fractionally and then nodded. Eduardo stepped off to the side, hoping the doctor would talk openly if he didn't appear to be eavesdropping.

It worked. "Looks like she dodged a bullet,"

the doctor said cheerfully. "Of course, we'll do a few more tests. CT scan as a precaution. But it looks like a very mild concussion. She has a few contusions, but we were able to patch her up. It could have been much worse."

"Can she go home tonight?"

The doctor frowned. "What's the home situation?"

"She has four kids."

"Then definitely not. She needs as much rest as possible, not a bunch of kids hanging on her. Besides, we need to do those tests. But she should be good for tomorrow." The doctor turned and hurried back into the ER.

"Thank you!" Daisy called after the doctor, sounding jubilant.

"You can go back and see her now," the receptionist said. "Just push the button to the right of the doors."

Daisy went over and pressed the button. The doors opened.

She looked back at him. "Come on," she said. "You can say you're my husband."

Reflected in the metallic doorway, he could see the flashing lights of an ambulance. Medics jogged in beside a stretcher holding a small dark-haired woman.

The beeps of medical machinery shrilled over

the low hum of voices, artificially calm doctors and nurses.

Behind him, in the waiting room, a child began to cry.

A roaring started in his head. *Your fault. Your fault. Your fault.*

That crying child sounded just like Sofia had sounded all those years ago, crying for the mommy who would never return.

What had he been doing, getting involved with Fiona and her family? Why would he risk replicating that kind of misery? What had possessed him, thinking he'd changed?

He'd come to care for Fiona and her kids way too much. Which was exactly why he needed to stay out of their lives.

He stepped back from Daisy's beckoning arm. "It's okay. Uh, you'll take care of her. Right?"

Daisy cocked her head to one side and looked at him hard. "Right, of course. I'm her *friend.*"

"That…that's great. You let me know if you need anything. Right now, I'm… I have to go. Go home."

He turned and practically ran out of the hospital.

Three days later, Fiona pushed herself up to a sitting position and readjusted her pillows behind her back. She was in her own sunny front room, waiting for the kids to come home from school, while Lou Ann Miller prepared dinner in the kitchen. The nanny, temporarily rehired, was playing with Poppy upstairs.

She looked out the window, relieved that the light didn't hurt her eyes today. The tests had all come back clear, and her slight dizziness had subsided. A faint lingering headache and some blue-green bruises up one arm were the only reminders of the fright she'd had last weekend. If she got lots of extra rest this week, and resumed her normal life slowly, she'd be fine, according to the doctors.

She was still a little hazy on the details of the accident. She remembered running out into the storm, not seeing her kids, thinking there was movement down by the water. Poppy had been so fascinated with Mercedes's story about hiding under the boat, and Fiona had feared that Poppy, or all her kids, were playing there or hiding from the lightning. Exactly the most unsafe thing to do.

She remembered looking around frantically, seeing the rowboat and then…just a big blank.

Sometimes, she got a mental glimmer of strong arms lifting her up and carrying her through the rain. It must have been Eduardo. She knew he'd driven her to the hospital while Daisy had held her steady in the back seat. Sam and Susan had taken all the kids home, got them dry clothes and food and reassurance. Other than Poppy being a little more clingy than usual, there were no ill effects.

Every time she thought about the near disaster, she closed her eyes and sent up a prayer of thanks and gratitude for the help of her friends.

The only thing missing now was Eduardo.

The school bus chugged up and her older three ran inside. She could hear the thuds and clinks of supplies as they threw down their backpacks and lunchboxes and then all three burst into the front room, Lauren importantly hushing everyone else.

Fiona hugged each one of them fiercely and made them sit around her and tell her about their school days. Maya had a drawing that had gotten two gold stars, Ryan had aced his spelling test and Lauren's oral report had gone "okay, better than Tiffany Winthrop's." Fiona listened and breathed in the sweaty smell of her kids, and again her heart expanded with thanks.

So easily, things could have gone a different way. She could have gotten a much worse concussion. *Even been killed.* The doctors had impressed on her the dangers of being outside in a lightning storm, and Fiona took it all seriously. More than ever, she felt grateful for each moment with her children and was determined to give them everything she had to help them grow up strong.

She wanted to get up and fix them a snack right now, as she usually did, but Lou Ann called out for them to come to the table. One mention of fresh-made brownies and Ryan and Maya ran toward the kitchen. Lauren stayed behind, leaning against Fiona.

Fiona held her hand as the others raced away, smiled at her eldest and brushed her hair back from her forehead. There were two vertical wrinkles between Lauren's eyebrows, a sure sign that something was wrong. "Come sit on the porch with me after you have your snack, if you want to."

Lauren glanced toward the kitchen, from which a rich chocolaty smell was wafting.

"Go ahead. Eat your snack and I'll meet you on the porch."

Lauren leaned down and gave Fiona a gentle hug. "Thanks, Mom."

Moments later, they were on the porch in the sun, both sipping iced tea, Lauren's watered-down with a significant amount of lemonade.

"Mom," she asked, "how come Mr. Delgado hasn't been over to visit like all your other friends?"

Fiona looked involuntarily in the direction of the carriage house. That was the million-dollar question, but she couldn't say that to her daughter. "I'm sure they've had a lot to do," she said. "And remember, Mr. Delgado has a landscaping business. Spring is his busiest season."

"Sofia says he's *moody*." Lauren looked rather impressed with her ten-year-old friend's observation. "She says he stares off into the distance. And he keeps looking at pictures of their mom, who died."

Fiona's heart was open and emotional and the idea of Eduardo, sad and suffering, pained her. But she'd sent him a note thanking him for rescuing her and for helping with the kids, along with Sofia's stain-free shirt. The ball was in his court now, but apparently he wasn't going to hit it.

"Sometimes grown-ups go through hard times, just like kids do," she said, feeling her way. "He could be feeling extra sad about losing his wife. Just like you sometimes get sad about Daddy, right around Christmas or your birthday."

"Yeah, because he used to get me lots of presents and call me his little lady." Lauren looked wistful.

"He loved you very much." Lauren, more than the others, had memories of Reggie. Sometimes Fiona speculated that Reggie hadn't yet started up his other family when Lauren was small, so he'd been more attached to her.

A car pulled up in front of the house and a petite dark-haired woman emerged. Fiona waved a greeting and started to stand, but the woman was looking past the house, where Eduardo soon appeared. He walked to meet the woman and they embraced.

Then they walked back toward the carriage house, arms around each other. Neither one glanced in the direction of the porch.

Lauren looked over at Fiona. "Does Mr. Delgado have a new girlfriend?" she asked.

Fiona's own automatic thought as well. She took a couple of deep breaths and thought about Eduardo, the man she knew him to be. Thought about how he'd expressed feelings for her and kissed her not even a week ago. "I don't think so, honey," she said. "That might be a relative."

And tried to hold on to her reasoning in the face of some very nasty jealousy.

"Oh, good," Lauren said matter-of-factly, "because we want you and Mr. Delgado to get married."

Fiona sighed, reached out and stroked Lauren's hair. "That's not going to happen, I'm pretty sure," she said softly.

"But you kissed him—"

"I know. We like each other. But when you're

a grown-up with jobs and kids and…and hard things that happened in the past, it's complicated to go on dates and to, well, be together." She chose her next words carefully, wanting to reassure Lauren and avoid making her feel somehow responsible or guilty. "I can only take care of so much. You and your sisters and brother fill up my world. You're my priority, and I wouldn't have it any other way. Do you understand?"

Lauren frowned. "That lady is really small and skinny. Do you think he likes her because she is littler than you?"

Fiona's breath caught as her daughter articulated the ugly notion that had stabbed at her the moment she'd seen Eduardo put his arm around the dark-haired woman. "What makes you think that, honey?"

"I know you go on diets, and in pictures, you hunch down to be smaller. So I thought…" She trailed off, looking at the floorboards of the porch.

Fiona lifted her eyes to the ceiling and tried to channel Daisy and Susan. "Sometimes, in magazines and on TV, women and girls look skinny and small. But that's not real life, is it? We come in all sizes."

Amazing how calm she was able to sound, as if she had complete confidence in these ideas that she was only now starting to internalize.

Amazing how important it felt now to correct her daughter's misperceptions, when she'd suffered under the same ideas herself for so many years.

"Tiffany Winthrop is the littlest girl in the class, and the prettiest, too. She teases me about being the biggest." Lauren studied the floor as if something very interesting was down there.

Hot anger rose in Fiona and she took a couple of breaths, then scooted over on the porch swing and put an arm around Lauren. "I'm sorry that's happening. It can't feel good."

"It doesn't. And now some of the other kids are saying it, too, and I'm afraid I won't have any friends." She looked up at Fiona. "Do you think I could go on a diet?"

Fiona swallowed a knot in her throat and tightened her arm around her daughter. "No way. You eat a normal amount, and you're a normal size. That's healthy." She focused on what Lauren had said, thought of how important Susan and Daisy were in her own life. "Let's think of all the good friends you have."

"Well, there's Dana. She's my best friend."

"I like Dana." And Fiona resolved to invite the girl over within the next week. "Who else?"

"Valerie and Danica and Annalisa and Beth. We all sit together at lunch."

"And they all came to your birthday party last year. They seem to really like you."

"And Sofia. She's not in my class, but we're friends at soccer. And at home." Lauren's face was brightening. "And David. He's a boy, but he's nice and fun. And he's a *lot* taller than I am."

"Boys can be good friends, too."

"He yelled at the boys who were teasing me. And Annalisa told the teacher."

Where had *she* been while her eldest was going through mean-girl misery? "I'm sorry all this has been happening. Why didn't you tell me?"

"Because I knew you'd get upset and talk to the school," Lauren said truthfully. "And anyway, you have to stay in bed."

Bad mother. Bad mother. The usual negative voices rose inside her, but alongside them, there was a core of strength that told her to look at the whole situation before she blamed herself.

Lauren and her friends were handling the name-calling. And Lauren was telling Fiona all about it now.

"You have some really good friends, it sounds like. Did you speak up to Tiffany when she said mean things?"

Lauren looked down again. "Yeah, but…"

"But what, honey?" She stroked Lauren's hair gently.

"I said mean things back to her. I called her a pip-squeak and I teased her about her bad grades."

Fiona nodded, watching emotions play across Lauren's face. Let her think it through.

"What should I do, Mom?"

"Would you feel better if you apologized?"

Barely, almost imperceptibly, Lauren nodded.

"Tomorrow?"

"Okay, Mom."

"Good." Fiona squeezed Lauren's shoulders again. "And I think it's time you started having more sleepovers. You and your friends are big enough to clean up after yourselves and fix your own snacks. Would you like to have two or three girls over? Not this week, since it's going to be Easter, but maybe next?"

"I'd love that!" Lauren hugged Fiona. "Can we make s'mores?" Then her face fell. "Oh, wait, are they fattening?"

Fiona took a breath. "Do you care? Since you're a normal weight and treats are part of good healthy eating?"

"We could have s'mores and strawberries," Lauren decided. "Okay?"

"Sure, as long as you share with the other

kids." She smiled at her thoughtful eldest daughter. "And me. I love strawberries *and* s'mores."

"Can I go call the girls now?"

"Sure thing." After Lauren ran inside the house, Fiona sat rocking and wondering whether she could take to heart her own wise words to her daughter.

"So what's this I hear about a new girlfriend?" Sara, Eduardo's sister-in-law, grinned at him and crushed her empty soda can before tossing it into the trash. They were sitting in Eduardo's little kitchen, catching up on the latest news about each other, the kids and their relatives. Except for her short hair and boyish T-shirt and jeans, she looked almost exactly like Elizabeth. Seeing her always provoked a mixture of joy and sadness in Eduardo.

"No new girlfriend," he said.

Sara raised an eyebrow. "Then who were you kissing on the street? Some random stranger?"

Eduardo let his head fall back against his chair and stared up at the ceiling. "How do you hear all the Rescue River gossip when you're living in Toronto?"

"I have my sources." She smiled. "And I want you to know that I think it's time. Elizabeth would, too."

"No." He watched the ceiling fan blades going

around. Was that a cobweb up there in the rafters? He'd have to get out a long-handled broom and get it down.

At the screen door, there was a scratching sound, and Sparkles stood up with a little lurch and made her way over. Outside, Brownie whined an invitation. Sparkles looked back over her shoulder at Eduardo, as if asking permission to go play.

He stood, glad for a reason to move away from Sara's intensity, and opened the door. "Go ahead," he said, running a hand along the dog's bony back as she went out. Brownie lowered his front half into a play bow and barked, then dashed away, and Sparkles followed at a more sedate lope.

He returned to the kitchen table to find Sara looking at him steadily. "Why not start dating? You're a normal man with normal feelings and needs. And those kids in there—" she gestured toward the living room, where Sofia and Diego had reluctantly gone to start their homework "—they would benefit from a woman's influence, especially now. Sofia's turning into a young lady."

Maybe it was because of Fiona's accident and his subsequent realization that he had fallen in love with her. Or maybe it was how much he missed talking to her. Something, at any rate, took away his usual filters. "Truth?" he said. "I'd like to date. And there's someone I have in mind, yeah. But after what happened with Elizabeth—"

"You're afraid of losing another wife?"

"I'm afraid of *letting down* another wife." He propped his elbows on his knees and leaned forward, staring at the floor. "You know all the troubles we had with insurance and doctors. If I'd had a better job, gotten her better care…" He trailed off and let out a sigh.

"Then what?" Sara asked gently.

"If I'd gotten better care for her, she might have survived."

Sara didn't say anything. What could she say?

After a minute, he hazarded a glance at her and saw that she was frowning and biting her lip.

"What?" he asked. "You can say it." He waited for the recriminations he'd always expected but had never received from Elizabeth's closest sister.

"I really shouldn't," she said. "But…" She looked away.

Diego came and knocked on the kitchen door frame. "Can Aunt Sara come play with us now?"

"In a minute, *chico*," she said. She got up and handed him two cookies from the plastic container she'd brought. "One for you and one for your sister," Sara said and ruffled his hair. For a minute, she looked so much like Elizabeth that Eduardo's throat tightened up.

But there was a surprising bit of happiness there, too. For once, he flashed on a memory of Elizabeth's life, not her terrible death—a time when she'd mussed up Sofia's hair in the exact same way, before she'd gotten sick.

"Thanks, Aunt Sara." Diego clearly didn't have any such complicated reaction. He just hugged her hard and then ran into the other room.

Sara turned back to Eduardo, leaned against the counter and crossed her arms. "I'm going to tell you something I wasn't supposed to tell you."

"About Elizabeth?"

She nodded. "I think you need to hear it. And I think Elizabeth would agree, if she knew how much you're beating yourself up."

He should tell her not to break Elizabeth's confidence, but the chance to hear something new about his wife was too intriguing. "Go on."

Sara drew in a breath and let it out in a big sigh. "She knew she was terminal from the very beginning."

Eduardo frowned, shook his head. "No, she didn't."

Sara walked over and sat down across the

table from him. "She just didn't want you and the kids to know."

"But the doctors never told me—"

"She didn't give permission," Sara said. "Medical records are private."

"She wouldn't have lied to me." Heat rose in him. He looked out the window and then back at Sara. "Would she?"

Sara reached out and clasped his hand. "Only if she thought it was the best for you. She knew how hard you'd take it. She knew you needed to fight."

Eduardo shook his head, trying to sort out the conflicting information. All the months of trying so hard to get her the best healthiest food, to enroll her in clinical trials, to research alternative treatments... Elizabeth had *known* it wasn't going to work, and she'd let him do it?

Painful anger battered at his heart. "But she told you? You, and not me?"

Sara sighed. "She had to talk to someone. I was the only person she told, and she made me promise not to tell you." She looked heavenward. "I'm sorry, *mi hermana*, but I have to break that promise. He needs to know."

"She couldn't talk to her own husband?"

Sara shook her head, shrugged and lifted her hands, palms up. "Some things you can only tell a sister. But the point is, Eduardo, you're not at fault for some imagined mistake you made in providing care for her. She wasn't going to beat her cancer."

She wasn't going to beat her cancer. She hadn't beat it. And she'd known she wouldn't from the beginning.

"Daddy," came Sofia's wheedling voice from the doorway, "can I go out and play with Lauren? I got almost all my homework done. And she said she needs to talk to me."

"Sure. Go. Your brother can go out, too." Normally, he would've looked into her claim further before letting her go, but he was still reeling from Sara's revelation.

After Sofia and Diego were outside, he scraped a hand across his face and looked at Sara. "How could Elizabeth have lied to me, even when she was so sick?"

She stood up instantly, came over and wrapped her arms around him from behind. "She agonized about it. Prayed about it. She didn't want to lie to you, but she loved you so much and she truly thought it was what would help you get through." She released him and sat back down. "For the record, I thought she should tell you the truth. But she felt like it was the last gift she could give you and the kids. Hope."

He shook his head. "Wow."

"She loved you so much. You know that, right?"

"Yeah." But processing what his sister-in-law had told him might take some time.

Sara hopped up and tugged at his hand. "Come on. Let's sit outside and watch the kids play and talk about something else. I've only got an hour before I have to get back on the road for my rally, and I want to take some pictures of those beautiful kids."

"I'm coming, I'm coming." He stood up and forced his attention out of the past and into the present, this sunny day, the opportunity for his kids to see the aunt they loved.

"Who's the older lady talking to Sofia and her friend?" Sara asked from the doorway. "They look like they're plotting something."

Eduardo glanced out the window. "That's Lou Ann Miller. She babysits for a lot of the kids in town when she can find the time between her athletics and her coursework." And she was helping Fiona while she recovered from her concussion. As he should have been doing, if he were more of a friend than a coward.

"Impressive. She's no spring chicken." Sara was still looking out the screen door. "FYI, it looks like Diego and another boy his age are getting involved in the plotting. You're probably going to be asked to spring for pizza, at the very least."

But as it turned out, the plot wasn't anything to do with pizza.

Chapter Eleven

Fiona sighed and stretched and looked at her watch. Cleveland's Gribshaw House Bed-and-Breakfast was beautiful, and she'd gotten lots of rest, but she didn't like being away from her children for more than twenty-four hours.

She shouldn't complain. The group of elders from the Senior Towers had been lovely to go together and get her this escape, all because they'd heard from Lou Ann that it was hard for her to rest when she was at home with four kids. What they didn't understand was that she didn't want to rest anymore. She felt fine. She wanted to go about her normal activities, cook and garden and take care of her children.

Even though the doctors said she should still take it easy, she was ready to jump into her life again.

She carried her overnight bag downstairs and

said goodbye to Mrs. Gribshaw, the proprietor, who'd been very kind…and extremely interested in everything about Fiona.

"You get help with those four children, you hear? Don't let them run all over you. When my kids were young, I traded mornings with my neighbor so I could get things done. You should try that."

"What a good idea," Fiona said. "Thank you for everything."

"You're welcome. You ought to think about eating more for breakfast, too, dear. There's nothing like a good breakfast to get you started in the morning. Gives you energy and pep. It's the most important meal of the day!"

"You're right," Fiona said, "and the breakfast was delicious." And massive. There had been only a few guests in the B and B last night, but Mrs. Gribshaw seemed to have cooked for a battalion. In point of fact, Fiona had eaten a big plate of eggs, bacon, toast and fruit for brunch and still felt full even though it was midafternoon. "Thank you again. I'd better get outside. My friend Susan is picking me up, and she's always in a hurry."

"Of course, dear," Mrs. Gribshaw said, a broad smile creasing her friendly face.

Fiona escaped into the cool morning air to the garden that surrounded the B and B. The treetops were filled with birdsong, and green hedges sat on either side of benches and along flagstone paths, and the flower beds were overflowing with what seemed like hundreds of daffodils.

She sank down onto a stone bench and lifted her face to the sunshine and thanked God, again, for all His blessings: health and safety for herself and her children; friends who cared enough to provide her with a vacation day; and a beautiful, natural oasis in the midst of a bustling city.

"Fiona?"

The familiar voice sounded a little disbelieving.

"Eduardo?" She turned, and there he was, framed in the arbor-style gateway to the garden. Involuntarily, she stood and walked toward him. "What are you doing here?"

"I could ask you the same question," he said slowly, his eyes narrowing. "Were the Senior Matchmakers involved in your being here?"

"Yes, they were," she said slowly. "They raised money for me to have a night off from mothering. I got a lot of rest last night, and it was great, but… Susan was supposed to come and pick me up today."

"And I was supposed to be picking up Susan here, because she was stranded."

Mrs. Gribshaw hurried out. "Oh, mercy, he's just as handsome as the ladies told me he'd be.

Dear me, but I had a hard time keeping this a secret. Here. I was to give this to you when your ride arrived." She held out a small gift bag to Fiona.

"What?" Fiona took the bag and stared at it, then at Mrs. Gribshaw, then Eduardo. "Who gave you this?"

"A whole carload of senior citizens from your small town. My, what fun they were having!" She looked a little wistful. And then she clapped a hand to her forehead. "And they specifically told me to leave you two alone while you opened it. Enjoy yourselves! Come back again soon!" She turned and practically scurried into the guesthouse.

Fiona watched her go and then looked at Eduardo, who was shaking his head.

"You'd better open it," he said, his voice resigned.

She did. "It's a gift card for dinner out at… Let's see. Ever heard of Bocca Felice in Little Italy?"

His eyebrows lifted. "Sure have. It's one of the best Italian restaurants in Cleveland. Is there a card?"

She took it out and read aloud, "'All of your kids are safe and happy with Lou Ann, Susan and Daisy. They'll be sound asleep when you get home. Enjoy a lovely evening.'" She looked at him helplessly. "What should we do?"

He shrugged. "Use it, I guess." He reached out for her overnight bag. "We'll put your bag in the car, and…" He checked the time on his phone. "It's a little early for dinner. Do you feel like walking?"

She was rapidly shedding her eagerness to get home in the face of spending time with Eduardo, even if it was togetherness forced by interfering friends. "I'd love to walk off Mrs. Gribshaw's breakfast if we're going to have a big Italian dinner."

"How are your shoes?" he asked, and she held out her foot to display her eminently practical rubber-soled canvas slip-ons.

"We'll drive over to this trail I know around the Lake View Cemetery. It's right by Little Italy. Have you been there?"

She shook her head, feeling a bit dizzy at how this day was shaping up. "Actually, beyond a little shopping, I haven't spent much time in Cleveland."

"You haven't seen the grave of the man who invented Salisbury steak?" he asked and held out a hand. "Come on. You're in for a cultural experience."

A wave of warmth toward him washed over her. He was such a good sport, and so much fun.

But was he just being kind? His day had been just as disrupted as hers had been. "Don't you have to work?"

"Normally, yes," he said, touching the small of her back to urge her toward his car. "But... Oh, man. Sam gave me the afternoon off so I could help Susan." He rolled his eyes and shook his head.

"They're all in on it!" Heat rose in her face. "Eduardo, I'm really sorry they're trying to push us together. Believe me, I had nothing to do with this."

"Nor did I. We have some interfering friends, for sure." He opened the car door for her. "Come on. Since they've gone to all this trouble, let's have some fun. We can pick up with our at-home lives at midnight."

"Like Cinderella," she said.

"Like Cinderella." He flashed her a smile as he closed the door, and all of a sudden, it felt like a real date.

Don't get carried away, Fiona.

They strolled the trail that looped around the historic cemetery, weaving through woods and low hills, and he regaled her with tales of life in the landscaping business. He'd had many funny customers and he was a good storyteller.

"Are you going to tell stories about the job on

my garden once it's all over?" she asked. "About this crazy lady with four kids who couldn't even understand the estimate you made?"

He reached out and took her hand, squeezed it, his face going serious. "I would never make fun of you for a disability."

"Guess what!" She turned to him, excited to remember her news. "I made an appointment to get tested. I'm coming back to Cleveland next week to meet with the specialist."

"Good for you."

"I know, and I owe it to you for bringing it up to me. So thank you."

"I'm glad I could help."

They were being polite and friendly with each other. It felt like they were on a first date. Not like they'd ever kissed...

Fiona looked across the trees to Lake Erie in the distance, and she tried to keep hold of the strength she'd found in her talks with her girl-friends and in her prayers.

I don't have to be defined by a man's views of how I should be. I'm strong in myself.

But her heart and mind kept skittering back toward Eduardo.

He was so very attractive. And kind and good-natured, getting into the spirit of a forced date planned not by him but by their friends. A lot of men would have been irritated at the unexpected change to their work schedule, but Eduardo cheerfully pointed out landscapes and held back branches and helped her over rough spots in the trail.

It was almost hard to remember that he'd been clear about what he wanted, and it wasn't her.

She was going to enjoy this one night with him, though. It had been kind of their friends to set this up, even if it wasn't going to go the way her heart wanted it to. She was going to live every day fully—that was one of the revelations she'd had in last night's solitude.

They came to a stretch of trail that ran through the woods, cool and refreshing. "I've been doing all the talking," Eduardo said. "Tell me about the B and B. How was it, getting a night away from the kids?"

"I miss them like crazy," she admitted. "But I took advantage of the time. Brought my Bible and did a lot of thinking and praying."

He glanced over at her as they walked side by side on a wide stretch of the trail. "About what, if you don't mind my asking?"

Fiona wasn't one to talk a whole lot about her faith. She'd grown up in a family that was private and restrained. But what did she have to lose? If nothing else, Eduardo was a member of her faith community and she knew they shared the same basic values.

"Death and resurrection," she said. "Don't laugh! I know it sounds super deep."

"I wouldn't laugh at your faith! Why do you think I would?"

Why *did* she think so? Immediately, the answer came to her: Reggie. "My husband was a churchgoer—liked to have me and all the kids dressed up nice and sitting in a row beside him—but when it came to talking about real faith, he brushed my ideas aside."

"That was wrong of him," Eduardo said sharply. "What's more, death and resurrection are the core of Christianity."

"True, but I didn't come up with the concept on my own. I've been doing a Lenten devotional… Well, when I have time…and I caught up on it last night. And it's one of those you apply to your own life, so… I did."

"Figure anything out?"

She looked at him shyly. "A couple of things. You sure you want to hear this?"

He squeezed her hand. "I want nothing more than to hear it," he said. And the look in his warm brown eyes told her he was being truthful.

What would it be like to be with a man who welcomed discussions that went beyond life's surface?

Be in the moment, Fiona. "Okay, here goes. Sometimes, I feel sorry for myself."

"You make that sound like such a bad thing. Who doesn't?"

"Well, you lost your wife…"

"And you lost your husband."

"But you had a great marriage. That must make it harder."

"In some ways," he said. "But your burden has been pretty heavy. You struggled through a tough marriage and then found out you'd been betrayed. You kept it together with four kids, and you're a fantastic mother to them."

She started to protest and he touched a finger to her lips, just one tiny touch, but it stole her breath. "No. Uh-uh," he said. "You're a fantastic mother, and I know that doesn't come easy. You end up sacrificing a lot of your own time and interests."

"Nothing could be more worth it."

"Agreed. But that doesn't mean it's easy." He dropped her hand and she felt bereft, but then he put an arm around her. "Is this okay?"

Her heartbeat skittered, then settled into a faster-than-usual rhythm.

Her cautious side told her to cool it. But this was just for one night. She could enjoy the dream for one night, right? She smiled up at him. "I like it."

He tightened his grip marginally, held her

gaze for a moment and then smiled a little and looked away, shaking his head.

What was he thinking?

"I interrupted you," he said after a moment. "You were starting to say you felt sorry for yourself. I had to argue, but I shouldn't have cut off your story."

She had to pause a moment to even remember what they were talking about. "It's fine. It's just that I was reading the Easter story. I always avoid it, you know. I hate to hear about how horribly everyone treated Jesus. And it just hurts that He was scared, and His disciples wouldn't stick by Him. But last night, I read it. I did what my devotional said and read it in all four gospels."

"Tough material."

"Yes, it was. But it brought something home to me. In addition to the fact that nothing I've suffered has any comparison to what He endured."

"That's true," he said quietly.

"But I also really took it in, for the first time, that even though He suffered horribly, the outcome was greater. It was greater because of His pain. And then that led me to the book of Romans, and the part about how suffering produces endurance and... Well, anyway, I'm talking too much."

"Fiona." His hand squeezed her shoulder. "I really want to hear it."

Around them, squirrels darted from branch to branch, and birds sang a quiet accompaniment. A rich pine scent rose from the forest floor. Now that they were deeper into the trees, there was a chill in the air, and Fiona was glad for Eduardo's warm arm around her.

Don't focus on that. "It's just… I realized that all my family went through, all the dark nights, all the tears…they're for some kind of purpose. They're a crucible, you know? They make us who we are. And they make us strong."

He tightened his arm around her shoulders, and this time, he didn't loosen his grip. "You're a very insightful person," he said.

"I'm not." She waved a hand and then looked up at him. "Do you think any of that applies to you?"

"That suffering's a crucible? I don't know." He frowned. "I spent a lot of time wondering why Elizabeth had to die. Listening to my daughter crying for her mama, knowing there was nothing I could do to help. It's hard to maintain your faith in that situation."

"Did you lose it?"

"For a time," he said. "I was really angry at God. Elizabeth was so good. She didn't deserve to suffer. But lately…" He trailed off.

"What?"

"Lately, I've been picturing her actually in heaven. She loved to sing, and so… Well, I've been imagining her singing in the heavenly choir. Is that weird?"

"I think it's beautiful." And it actually choked her up a little. She cleared her throat. "Does it make you feel better?"

He nodded. "My anger is really sort of selfish. It's about me. Because she's fine. She's happier than ever, filled with joy."

She nodded, and just for a moment, she felt sad for Reggie. "I'm sorry to say I don't have that confidence about my husband." She took a breath. "But my pastor back in Illinois said to leave it in God's hands, that maybe Reggie had turned it around in the last moments. I hope he did."

"That's because you're a good person."

She looked off into the trees and shook her head. "No. Not really. But I'm glad you're figuring out how to deal with losing your wife. Did you share the choir image with Diego and Sofia?"

"No, I didn't. But maybe I will."

They'd come out of the park and into Little Italy, a colorful old street full of turreted brick buildings, restaurants, shops and a beautiful church as an anchor. The sun shone gold through a partly cloudy sky. Couples and clusters of young people, talking and laughing, gave the street a bustling air.

It's just for this one night, Cinderella, she reminded herself. Eduardo was honorable, trustworthy, able to talk about his feelings, a great father, a faithful Christian. He was still a man, though, and she couldn't quite shake the notion that men weren't to be trusted, that she wasn't good enough for a man like Eduardo.

Just for this one night, though, she'd enjoy the fairy tale.

As they walked into Bocca Felice, Eduardo had a moment of misgiving. This was the type of restaurant he'd been to maybe twice in his life—all white tablecloths, attentive waiters and well-dressed people talking quietly. He appreciated the seniors' gesture, but he felt out of place.

Fiona, on the other hand, lived in this world. She could probably write a check tonight to buy the whole building if she wanted to.

Sure enough, she looked perfectly at ease as they waited to be seated. "The food smells fabulous. Let's ask if we can sit by the window and watch the people." Which they proceeded to do and discovered they both liked imagining the lives of the various groups, individuals and couples passing by. Fiona was friendly with the waiter, happy to try what he recommended, and she ate with gusto, which Eduardo found incredibly appealing.

The whole thing was pleasing. He was out on a date with Fiona Farmingham. He'd somehow gotten up the courage to put his arm around her, and she'd let him! The feel of her shoulders beneath his hand and arm seemed burned in his memory.

His usual warning to himself—that he shouldn't get close, that he was a bad risk—nudged at him. But suddenly, now, he questioned the concept.

If Elizabeth's death hadn't been his fault...and if, as Dion had said, they were saved and forgiven by Christ, which was what the cross was all about...then he was free.

Free to live without the horrible weight that had been pressing down on him for so many years.

Free to look at his kids without feeling responsible for the death of their mother.

Free to court Fiona, if she'd have him.

But why *would* she have him? He was still just a landscaper. He was in awe of a restaurant this expensive. He lived in the little carriage house behind her big house, which seemed to symbolize their relationship.

Except...she never ever made him feel like he

was less than her. She was a good person and didn't put so much stock in material things.

If she wasn't putting up barriers, then why should he?

After dinner, they strolled slowly through Little Italy. Streetlights and colorful signs lit up as the sun glowed red gold on its way into night. *Almost the color of Fiona's hair*, Eduardo thought and then half smiled to himself. He'd never been much of a romantic, but maybe, just maybe, that was changing.

"Why did you let me order the tiramisu?" Fiona groaned. She was holding his arm with one hand and her stomach with the other.

"Wasn't it delicious?" he asked. "Mine was."

"Yes, it was fantastic, but I overdid it."

"You didn't finish your lasagna," he said, holding up their doggie bag as evidence. "Besides, I like a woman who enjoys her food."

She glanced over at him, narrowing her eyes. "You don't have to say that."

He didn't look away. "Why shouldn't I say the truth?"

Color rose in her cheeks and she laughed a little. "Come on, let's walk."

Ahead of them, on the steps of the stately Holy Rosary Church, at least ten white-gowned brides stood around while two more posed on the steps.

Photographers called out orders and assistants scurried about.

"We have twenty minutes of decent light, max!" yelled a man in a suit. "I want everyone in position."

Fiona and Eduardo looked at each other, nodded agreement and joined the small crowd of onlookers.

"What's going on?" Fiona asked a woman next to her. "Not a group wedding, surely."

"Photo shoot for some bridal website," another man informed them. "They've been here for an hour and everyone's getting cranky."

One of the brides, along with a photographer, came to a railing in front of the small crowd.

"Folks, I'll need you to move away, please," an assistant said, tossing a cigarette butt to the ground.

In a jostling, unorganized way, the little crowd moved to get out of the camera's line of sight.

"Could ya hurry, Theo?" the bride said. "I'm starving and this dress is squeezing me like a sausage!"

Fiona laughed, along with several of the women. "I wouldn't wear such a tight dress if you paid me," a twentysomething woman said. "I want to enjoy my own wedding."

"When I got married," said a white-haired

woman, "poufs and ruffles were the style. They covered a multitude of sins."

"High-waisted prairie style for me," said a fiftysomething woman with long hair and a lot of turquoise jewelry. "Much more comfortable."

"You guys are killing me," the model called over. "Just whatever you do, don't start talking about food."

"Best ravioli in the world just up the street!" called a man with an Italian accent. "DeNunzio's Family Restaurant. You should come on up after."

"DeNunzio's *is* good," the white-haired woman agreed. "Served with that wonderful bread, isn't it?"

"You bet." The round balding man who'd brought up the restaurant was out of the crowd now, edging closer to the model. "Dripping with butter. All you can eat."

"You're cruel!" the model cried.

"And…shoot," the photographer said. "Turn. Chin up. Smile!"

"I'm there for you afterward," the balding man said.

"You're old enough to be her father!" someone catcalled.

The model laughed and pointed at the Italian man. "Just wait for me to change into sweats, and I'd love to go to dinner with you."

The man pumped his fist in the air and the crowd laughed.

Fiona was laughing along with everybody else and Eduardo loved watching her, so he was sorry when she turned to him with an expression of regret. "We should go, I guess," she said. "Though the romantic in me would love to stay and see whether they end up together."

"What was *your* wedding dress like?" he asked as they strolled on toward the car. Then, because he was feeling brave, he took her hand. He held his breath as he did it, but she gave his hand an answering squeeze and smiled over at him.

"I could identify with that model," she said. "I was a lot thinner then, but my mom still talked me into a dress that was a half size too small. Let's just say, there wasn't room for wedding cake."

"But you love dessert. Right?"

"Yep. And it shows." She glanced down at herself.

"You know what?" he said. "Men don't like women who are the size of those models, not really. Most of us like normal women who enjoy food. And life."

"You didn't see any plus-size models at that photo shoot, did you?"

"Those magazines and websites are for women,

not men. Women are the ones who focus on the skinny. It's not an issue for men." He smiled at her. "Not for me. Believe me. And besides," he said, "you talk like you're overweight, but you must be comparing yourself to a time when you were thin as a rail. You look wonderful now."

Two pink spots appeared on her cheeks. She looked at him and then away. "Thanks for saying that."

He pulled her to face him. "I'm not just saying it. It's true."

For a minute, he wanted to kiss her right there on the street, but she gave a tiny smile and tugged him to start walking again. "It's late. We should be getting home."

Their drive back to Rescue River was quiet. When they got to Fiona's property, he pulled into the parking space by the carriage house. "I'll walk you home."

"That would be nice," she said. "It's a lovely night."

And it was. Moonlight shone silver over the stone path that wound from the carriage house to the walkway of the big house. Apple blossoms and spring flowers released their scent to the warm night air. "Let's stop by the garden," he suggested. "I want to show you something."

"Yes! I haven't been out since my accident."

They got there, and Eduardo knelt and showed

her the inch-high sprouts. "Your peas and kale and chard are coming in now," he said, looking up at her.

She crouched beside him. "That was so fast!"

"Good soil and air and sunshine. That's all a plant needs to grow."

She met his eyes and studied him thoughtfully.

Could their relationship grow, too? Did they have what was needed to make it thrive?

He reached for her, moved closer. "I don't want this evening to end," he admitted.

"It's been lovely," she said, her voice guarded. "The seniors were so sweet to set it up."

He reached for her face, ran a finger down her smooth cheek and leaned closer. But she pulled back a little.

"Come on, Eduardo. You're getting caught up in the date and the romance, but I know you don't want to take this further. You made it very clear."

"I've done some thinking since then," he said.

"Is that right?" Her voice was husky.

"Yeah." He leaned closer, but far enough that he could see her eyes. "I had a barrier related to some past baggage, but it's recently gotten knocked over."

She just looked at him, her eyes speculative.

"So I was wondering…if I can kiss you."

"Well…" She took a step back and looked up at the star-filled sky. "I don't want it to turn out badly again."

"I won't…"

"Because, Eduardo," she said in a low, intense voice, "that really hurt."

"I'm sorry." He cupped her cheek in his hand gently. "That's the last thing I want to do, hurt you. And if you're not interested, that's okay, too."

"I'm interested. But cautious."

"Understandable." He stood up and held out his hand to pull her to her feet.

"Come on, I'll walk you home."

"You're not mad?"

He shook his head. "How could I be? I want the best for you. And I respect your feelings."

They strolled slowly toward the house, holding hands. They weren't talking, but the silence was comfortable. And it wasn't really silence, because the crickets' chorus serenaded them, rising and falling. Freshly plowed earth from the field next door mingled with blossoms Fiona had planted around the base of her flowering trees.

The aroma of spring.

They were almost to her house now, and he dropped her hand to slide an arm around her back. He couldn't help wanting to be closer to her.

Her steps slowed, then stopped. She turned to face him.

"Too much?" he asked, lifting his hands away from her. The last thing he wanted to do was to push her or overstep her boundaries.

"No, not too much." She stepped closer and put her arms around him, so he let himself hold her. It felt like a precious gift.

She lifted her face to his. "About that kiss…"

He looked down at her and lifted an eyebrow. "Yeah?"

She slid a hand up into his hair and pulled his face down to hers. And then he was kissing her soft lips, and the emotion of it, the closeness, the sense of possibility almost knocked him out.

Until he heard a door open behind him.

"Fiona!" said a high female voice. "What on earth are you doing?"

Chapter Twelve

"You're making macaroni and cheese for lunch?" Fiona's mother swept into the kitchen the next day in a swirl of her trademark perfume.

"Uh-huh." Automatically, Fiona sucked in her stomach. She wished her mother hadn't decided to surprise them by visiting early.

"What are *we* going to eat?"

Fiona stirred cheese into the white sauce. "I can make extra salad if you don't want the carbs, Mom."

Poppy ran into the room and Fiona welcomed the distraction. "My mommy!" her youngest crowed and flung herself against Fiona's leg.

"My Poppy!" Fiona echoed, sweeping her up.

Poppy chortled gleefully. It was a game she never tired of.

"You're going to hurt your back, picking up a three-year-old like that," her mother said.

Fiona cuddled Poppy closer and then set her down so she could stir the sauce. 'Believe me, after four kids, my back is strong."

Poppy ran to Fiona's mother. "My grammy!" she shouted and hugged her grandmother's leg.

"Oh, sweetie, I've missed you so much." Her mom's eyes softened as she cuddled Poppy against her leg. "Guess what? Grammy brought each of you kids a present. You can open them after lunch."

Poppy's eyes widened. "Really?"

"Really."

"Can I tell?"

"Of course you can, honey."

Poppy raced out of the room.

"That was nice of you, Mom." Her mother really did love her grandkids and missed them since they'd moved out of state. Even though Fiona had felt the move necessary for herself and her kids, being away from one of their only living relatives was a huge disadvantage. She vowed to plan a family trip to visit her mother once school was out.

In the den, Fiona could hear the kids laughing, balls bouncing and toys beeping and ringing, and her heart swelled with gratitude. She was so glad to be home and feeling better, taking care of her kids. It just took a little accident sometimes to remind you how precious every moment of daily life actually was.

Last night had been precious, too. Every time she thought of her evening with Eduardo, warm excitement expanded in her chest. The walk, the dinner, their conversation…his compliments… the way he accepted her as she was…the feeling of holding his hand. All of it filled her with such sweet promise.

The kiss had been wonderful, too. Until the unfortunate interruption by her mother.

To his credit, Eduardo hadn't seemed upset. He'd squeezed her shoulders and whispered, "Need me to stay?" And when she'd shaken her head, he'd quickly introduced himself to Fiona's mother, waved and headed home.

He was a grown-up. Which couldn't be said of some men she'd known.

"Is there something you're not telling me?" her mother asked. She was holding up a large hardback book, *Stage a Beautiful Barn Wedding*.

Fiona laughed. "It's not what you think, Mom." She checked the pasta. "Actually, I'm considering starting a business. I'd like to make the barn in the back field into a wedding venue."

Her mother's thin eyebrows rose to her perfectly coiffed hair. "Really?" She managed to put a world of skepticism and doubt into that single word.

Shouldn't have told her. Fiona straightened her shoulders and refocused on the food. "Yes, really." She turned off the cheese sauce and carried the pot of pasta over to the colander in the sink.

"You know, honey, it's great that you keep trying. But you have to acknowledge your limitations." Her mother's voice was quiet, worried.

The words made her think of a poster she'd seen in Daisy's social work office, festooned with butterflies and flowers. Something about learning to fly despite your limitations.

Her mother was from another generation. She didn't understand learning disabilities. And Fiona didn't have to buy into her mom's old-fashioned assessment.

Once the food was on the table and they'd said grace and started eating, Fiona's mother kept the conversation rolling with her grandkids, asking them questions about school and activities and friends. The kids ate up the attention, along with big plates of food.

Her mother picked at her salad and turned down the macaroni and cheese. "I don't dare. It does smell good, though."

Fiona didn't have much of an appetite, either. She was thinking about Eduardo and about starting her business, and anxiety nudged at her despite her efforts to avoid it. Was she smart enough to start a wedding business? Was she just making excuses, thinking she might have a learning disability?

Had Eduardo really felt something for her yesterday, or was he just being nice?

She tuned back into the conversation when her mother's tone changed. "My," she said, "you certainly do spend a lot of time with these Delgado children. Isn't that the man who was, ahem, *here* last night?"

"They're our best friends!" Maya said.

"Um-hum." Then her mother focused in on Lauren. "You don't have to finish all that," she said, pointing to Lauren's nearly empty plate. "It's never too soon to start watching your weight."

Fiona put her fork down. "Lauren is a healthy girl with a healthy appetite. She knows how to listen to her body. That's what we all try to do, right, kids?"

"Right, Mom," they chorused dutifully.

Lauren looked at Fiona, her face anxious.

"Go ahead, honey," she said to Lauren. "Eat what you're hungry for. There's plenty."

Lauren looked at the remaining food on her plate. "No, it's okay. I'm getting full."

"Good for you," Fiona's mother said.

"Mom." Heat rose in Fiona's face. She was used to her mother's jabs, had grown up on them, but no way was she going to let her mom start on her girls.

Her mother just took another small bite of salad.

"Hey, I'm done eating, too," Maya said.

"Me, too!" Poppy's fork fell with a clatter. "Presents, presents!"

Ryan blinked and pushed his own plate away. "Can we open them, Grammy?"

"Of course! Will you come help me carry them in?"

"Yeah!" He jumped up and ran toward the guest bedroom, then stopped to wait for his grandmother. Moments later, they were back in the kitchen, each carrying two wrapped presents.

"Youngest first, or oldest?" Lauren asked, looking at Fiona. Her voice sounded a little unhappy, probably because her gift was much smaller than the other three.

"Alphabetical order this time," Fiona said. She liked to try to mix it up. "Who goes first?"

"I do!" Lauren ripped into her present and her eyes widened. She pulled out the latest cell phone model. "Wow! Thank you, Grandma! Wow!" She ran around the table to hug her, then turned to Fiona. "Am I allowed to have this?"

"We'll talk about it," Fiona said, trying to conceal her inner groan. She'd had no intention of letting her kids have cell phones this young, but how was she supposed to retract a gift like that?

"I'll be the first girl in my class to have this model," Lauren crowed. "Even Tiffany doesn't have one! And I can't wait to show Sofia."

Fiona supposed they could load games onto the phone and put some kind of parental controls on it. "We'll have to figure out how you can use that," she warned. "There are going to be limits."

"I know. I'm just going to set it up to try it out. A little. Thank you, Grandma." Lauren kissed her grandma's cheek and then started playing with the phone, pressing buttons and studying the screen.

"Who's next in the alphabet?" Fiona smiled at Maya.

"*L*, then *M*! Me!" Maya ripped into her large package, but her forehead creased as she opened the box. Billows of taffeta burst out. She pulled out a long tutu, two leotards and ballet practice shoes. "But I don't dance, Grammy."

"Keep looking," her grandmother said, and Maya pulled out an envelope and opened it. "Gift…"

"Certificate," Lauren read over her shoulder. "For Miss Josephine's School of Dance. Where's that, Mom?"

"It's in Creeksville." Which was forty-five minutes away. Her mother must have forgotten Maya was anything but a ballet type of kid. "That was nice of you, Mom."

Maya shrugged. "I can try it," she said and hugged her grandmother. "Hurry up, you guys. I want to go out and play!"

"Poppy, it's your turn," Lauren said. "The big one's for you. Want me to help you?"

Poppy nodded, and they ripped into a giant fully stocked dollhouse. "Aww, look at all the little furniture," Lauren said. "This is so cool!"

Even Ryan and Maya came over to see. "Poppy, that's great," Maya said, squatting down to examine the furniture wrapped up inside. "Can I help you set it up later?"

Poppy looked around and seemed to realize that her present was desirable to everyone. She smiled broadly. "You can all play, but I'm the boss!"

"Tell Grammy thank you," Lauren coached, and Poppy ran over to fling herself into her grandmother's lap.

"Thank you, Grammy! I love my dollhouse!"

Fiona's mother smiled and hugged Poppy close. "I'm glad, sweetie."

Ryan ripped open his present next and his eyes went wide. "Look, Mom!"

Fiona came over and squatted to look at the enormous building kit. "That's a very generous gift," she said, knowing Ryan adored the movie series it was based on. "You'll love playing with that, buddy."

He thanked his grandmother and then ran back to study the carton.

The gift had surely cost several hundred dollars. All of them had. Fiona blew out a breath.

She tried not to emphasize money to her kids, had always done her best to keep the gifts modest at Christmas, focusing on the reason for the season. But you couldn't control what relatives wanted to give, and her children would enjoy what her mother had provided.

She'd figure out how to limit the phone use and handle the unwanted dance lessons after her mother left town.

"Isn't that the one Diego is always talking about?" Lauren sank down to her knees beside Ryan to look at the building kit.

"Yeah, he really wants one. But they don't have enough money to buy it. Hey, maybe I'll share this with him!"

Fiona's heart swelled with pride for her thoughtful son.

"That's the way to get the toy broken," her mother said. "Those people aren't careful with their things."

Fiona opened her mouth, but before she could speak up, Ryan did. "Do you know the Delgados, Grammy?" He sounded puzzled.

"Sofia and Diego are *really* careful with their toys," Lauren said.

"More careful than me," Maya added.

Before her mother could say anything else, Fiona started clearing dishes from the table. Lauren picked up a load, too, and Ryan reluctantly put aside his new treasure to pick up his plate and Poppy's.

"Thank you," she said. "If you kids will finish clearing the table and wipe it off, your grandma and I will do the dishes. You can play with your toys."

When she reached the sink, Fiona looked out the window and saw Eduardo working on the garden, putting up the fences he'd promised to keep unwanted critters out. His dark hair shone in the sunlight, and his muscles strained the sleeves of his shirt as he put the pickets into place. She felt a surge of happiness just seeing him.

Her mother came up beside her. "He's your *gardener*?"

"No, Mom," she said patiently. "He's an independent contractor. He does landscaping for people all over town."

"Do you think he's here legally? So many immigrants who don't have their papers work in landscaping."

"Mom! Of course he—"

"Oh, my goodness," her mother interrupted,

"I wonder if he's after a green card, romancing you."

Fiona frowned and looked pointedly toward the children, going in and out with dishes and sponges.

And ears tuned to adult conversation.

"I mean, that would make more sense of why he's paying attention to you," her mother said in a lower voice once the kids were out of the kitchen. "He's very good-looking."

Fiona wanted to put her hands over her ears to push out her mother's words, but even more, she wanted to correct the misperceptions. "Look, Mom, the Delgados are second-generation. Yes, they're of Mexican descent, but they're American citizens. And Eduardo isn't the type to use anyone, anyway."

"Hmm." Her mother opened the dishwasher. "Still, you'd think he'd want someone…smaller," she mused.

"I need a break from this conversation." Fiona let the pan she was washing slide into the soapy water, marched to the unoccupied front room and leaned against the wall.

She's always like this.

She's not going to change.

She doesn't define you.

The prejudice was unfortunate and meant she'd have to sit down with the kids and explain that their grandmother had some blind spots, that they should treat all people the same.

The idea of Eduardo preferring a tiny woman… That remark dug at her.

Eduardo had told her he liked the way she looked. They'd laughed together at the bride show and the model's complaints about being hungry.

But then again, his first wife had been tiny. He'd said so himself. *Tiny and pretty*, his kids had said.

But he likes me, he said so!

Of course, he'd say that. He's kind and gentle. He doesn't want to hurt anyone.

She sank down into a chair and looked absently at the bookshelves, trying to postpone the moment when she had to go back to her mother's company.

Her eyes settled on a diet book she'd bought a year ago during one of her low self-esteem periods. It was one of those fad diets, promising speedy weight loss. Not very healthy, and she'd never tried it. She should have thrown the book away.

Maybe it would work, though. And if she lost weight, she'd feel so much better about herself. Her mother would get off her case, and men wouldn't treat her the way her husband had.

She pulled it off the shelf.

* * *

Paperwork day. Eduardo didn't love it, but nobody wanted their landscaping done on Easter weekend, so it was a good time to catch up. Trouble was, the weather was gorgeous and he'd always rather be outside. The kids were already running around, and from the sounds of it, they'd connected with Fiona's kids, who were also out enjoying the beautiful spring weather.

Fiona. He'd texted her a *hello* this morning and had gotten no response. But she was probably busy with her surprise guest.

How had it happened that they'd kissed only two times, and they'd been caught on both occasions? Once by the kids, and once by her mother, and he didn't know which was worse. He hoped Fiona's mom hadn't been too hard on her.

After a few minutes of daydreaming about yesterday, he decided to take his laptop outside. Maybe he could concentrate better there, push aside the warm feeling that grew in him when he thought of spending yesterday with her, holding her hand, sharing stories that drew them ever closer as they got to know each other.

He'd barely settled himself on the front porch with his laptop and a glass of iced tea when he heard several of the kids come around the side of the house.

"Are you guys Mexicans?" Ryan was asking.

"Kind of," Diego said. "We're Americans, but our grandparents moved here from Mexico, so that's why we have darker skin and hair."

"Our grandma says *you people* don't take care of your things, but we told her you do," Maya said. "Hey, are you guys poor?"

Heat rose in Eduardo's neck, but he forced himself to stay seated and let Diego handle it.

"No!" Diego said, and then there were murmurs Eduardo couldn't make out. "I don't want to play with your building set, anyway," Diego said sharply. "I don't like it anymore."

More murmurs, then Diego spoke again. "He could buy it for me if he wanted to, but he doesn't want to."

From the opposite direction, Sofia came up onto the porch and sat by Eduardo. "Lauren got a phone," she said.

"Really?" That surprised him. He wouldn't have pegged Fiona as a person who'd buy her ten-year-old a cell phone, but maybe he didn't know her as well as he thought.

"I wish I could have one," Sofia said, "but it's okay, Dad. I know you don't have enough money for it."

He blew out a breath. His happy mood was rapidly disappearing.

A little later, after Sofia had taken off, Poppy came to the bottom of the porch steps and stood looking at him. That was surprising. She wasn't usually off on her own apart from the others.

And although she'd become more comfortable with him, he didn't want to scare her, so he stayed in his seat. "Hey, Poppy," he said, keeping his voice casual.

Slowly, she came to the top of the stairs and again stood still, looking at him. It was a little creepy.

"Anything wrong, honey?" he asked her. "Where's your mom?"

"It's okay if she marries you," Poppy said, taking a step closer, but holding on to the porch railing.

He couldn't help smiling. "We're not planning on that," he said, and then something made him add, "right now, anyway."

"If you marry Mommy, you won't have to go away," she explained seriously.

"We don't have to go away, sweetheart."

"Yes, you do, to Mex-i-co," she said in a sing-song voice and moved closer until she was right by his side. "Lauren and Ryan 'splained it to me. But if you marry Mommy, you and Sofia and Diego can stay." She studied him. "You can be my daddy."

The acceptance in that sweet smile warmed his heart, but the implications of what she'd said, in all innocence, annoyed him thoroughly. Who had been telling Poppy that Eduardo and his family were illegal immigrants?

"Thank you, Poppy," he said. "Now, you'd better run home."

As she went down the steps, Diego came running up, his face stormy.

"Whoa, son, what's wrong?"

"Leave me alone!" Diego hurried into the house.

Eduardo tried to focus on his work, to give Diego some space, but he'd never been very good at that, especially when one of his kids was obviously hurting. And the things Poppy had said kept playing in his mind. *Poor...you people...can't afford...not Americans...*

Sofia came up the steps again, looking glum.

"Hey, Sof, what's wrong?"

"Nothing."

"Come on." He patted the chair beside him. "Tell me."

She sat down and shrugged. "Now that Lauren has a phone, she's texting with all these other girls in our grade. She doesn't want to just, you know, hang out."

"That's a problem with cell phones." And it was one reason why he didn't think children should have them.

"I just wish we weren't poor," Sofia burst out. She stood and flounced into the house.

This had gone too far. Eduardo followed her, shaking his head, and called for Diego to come downstairs. Once they were both sitting on the couch, he nudged his way between them and put an arm around each.

"I love you both," he said, feeling his way, "and I can't stand it when other people say things to hurt you."

"We know, Dad." Diego tried to shift away.

"It sounds like someone has been talking about us being Mexican."

Sofia rolled her eyes. "Duh, Dad. I mean, it's obvious from how we look."

Eduardo frowned. Those didn't sound like words Sofia would have come up with on her own. But probing for details wasn't the answer. "I'm proud of my Mexican heritage, and so was your mom. So many artists and businesspeople and athletes come from—"

"We *know*, Dad!"

Okay. So now wasn't the time for a history lesson, but he still had more to say to his kids. "The other thing to remember is that it's not what you have that makes you good and important. It's what's in your hearts."

"Uh-huh," Diego said.

"Can we turn on the TV?" Sofia asked.

He sighed and took a good look at Sofia, then

at Diego. Not only did they look upset, but they both looked weary.

It was tiring when people took swings at your self-image. And maybe something he'd said would sink in later.

"Sure, okay," he said, standing up. "I'll be out on the porch if you want to talk."

No answer. As he walked outside, the TV blared behind him.

Eduardo sat, looking out over the grass, thinking.

Obviously, a lot of this new talk and negativity came from Fiona's mom. He couldn't blame Fiona for what her mother thought or said. He didn't know whether she agreed with any of it or not.

But he *did* know that Fiona could buy her kids anything they wanted.

If they blended their families, Fiona's mother would be a part of his life, and more important, a part of his kids' lives. They'd be exposed to attitudes he tried to protect them from. Exposed on a frequent basis, from an actual relative.

And there was another problem: his own kids would have far less materially than Fiona's kids would. And no matter how hard you tried to instill the right values in your kids, they were still kids. They wanted what other children had, especially those in their own families.

Other people would look at him and Fiona the way her mother did. Thinking he'd married her for money, or for a green card. The very idea made heat rise through his body, made his head feel like it was going to explode.

He couldn't live like that. Couldn't expose his kids to the poison. He had to protect his family; he'd vowed that he would.

He sat another half hour, thinking.

And then he got on the phone with the manager of the motel they'd stayed at before. Negotiated a good rate for an end room, where they wouldn't bother the other guests.

Now that he had an alternative place to live, though, something nagged at him. Some feeling that he wasn't doing the right thing.

Chapter Thirteen

Fiona had just started to recover from her mother's digs when Brownie went crazy with barking, and Fiona opened the front door to find Susan and Daisy, both wearing workout clothes. Their friendly faces looked like sunshine after a morning of grey clouds.

"Ready for our walk?" Susan asked.

"Shh, Brownie!" Fiona grabbed the dog's collar, looked back into the house and then frowned out at her friends. "I'd love to come," she said, "but Mom's visiting. I can't make it today. Didn't you get my text?"

"We *need* you." Daisy gave her a winning smile.

"Go find your walking shoes," Susan said and then added in a whisper, "I'll take care of your mom."

"Who is it, Fiona?" Her mother came into the

foyer, and her standard social smile appeared on her face. "Hello, ladies."

"Hi, Mrs. Farmingham!" Susan gently shoved Fiona to the side as she walked in, holding out a hand. "I didn't get a chance to chat with you when you got here last night."

"Oh, yes. The babysitter." Mom didn't hold out her hand, which was unusual for her. "Susan, right? I remember meeting you a while back, but I'm sorry I don't remember your last name. I have such trouble pronouncing… Well, it was a bit *unusual*, I think."

Susan didn't retract her hand, although her smile widened into something of a grimace. "That's right. Hayashi was my maiden name. But I'm married to Sam Hinton now. You know, the *head of Hinton Industries*. So I'm Susan Hinton now."

"Oh!" Now Fiona's mother's smile became more genuine, and she shook Susan's hand with warmth.

"Get your shoes!" Daisy nudged Fiona toward the stairs and then walked up to Fiona's mother. "And I'm Daisy *Hinton*, Sam's sister," she said sweetly. "I was babysitting the kids last night, too, but in the confusion I don't think we really exchanged names."

Fiona jogged upstairs, grabbed her workout shoes and sat at the top of the stairs to put them on. If her friends could get her an hour away from her mother's negative commentary, she'd buy them both enormous pastries at the Chatterbox.

And one for herself as well.

"I know how much you love your grandkids," Daisy was enthusing. "Fiona has said so much about all the nice gifts you send."

"So we thought we'd give you a little time alone with them, away from Fiona." Susan's voice was firm. "She has a hard time letting anyone else take charge."

"Come on, Fiona!" Daisy called gaily up the stairs. "We won't take no for an answer. Your mom wants the kids to herself."

Blinking, Fiona walked down the stairs. No way was her mom going to let herself be manipulated like this. But it would be *so* nice to escape…

Susan grabbed her arm. "Let's go. Bye, Mrs. Farmingham!"

"Mom?" Fiona looked over her shoulder at her mother as Susan pulled her out the door."

"Thanks so much for letting us steal her away!" Daisy had her hand on the doorknob. "Your grandkids are going to be thrilled!"

Her mother looked a little befuddled. "Well…"

"We'll be back by dinnertime," Susan called.

"In fact, we'll *bring* dinner. Don't want you to have to cook. Just enjoy the kids."

By *dinnertime*? Fiona looked at her phone. It was only two o'clock. Her mom couldn't…

"That'll be fine, I guess," her mom said in a faint voice.

"You're such a sweetheart!" Daisy said and closed the door behind them with a sharp click.

They walked down the porch steps and around the side of the house in silence, but once they were safely out of sight and earshot of Fiona's mother, Susan and Daisy high-fived each other.

"You guys, I can't go for a walk without telling the kids."

"I saw Lauren with a phone when we came in," Daisy said. "Why don't you just text her?"

"I don't want to encourage…"

"What's her new number?" Susan asked.

"I don't remember. I don't even want her to have a…"

"Did you put it in your phone?" Susan asked as they walked past the carriage house. She took Fiona's phone out of her hand and started scrolling.

Sparkles loped over on three legs, nudged Fiona's hand and whined.

"Are you looking for Brownie?" Fiona asked.

She gestured toward her house. "He's back there. Go get him."

Sparkles cocked her head as if trying to understand.

"Go get Brownie," Fiona said again, waving an arm toward her house.

The dog's tongue lolled out in a sort of smile, hanging to one side, and she ambled toward Fiona's house.

"Here, I found Lauren's number and I'm texting her," Susan said. "I'm saying, 'It's Mrs. Hinton. Congrats on new phone.'"

A few seconds later, Susan's phone buzzed and she read out Lauren's text:

So excited! Put you in my contacts!

"But I haven't even decided if I'm going to allow..." Fiona protested.

"Hey, there." Eduardo's voice sounded from the direction of the carriage house. Fiona's heart pumped harder as she looked over to see him jump nimbly off the side of the steps and walk toward them. "We need to talk," he told her.

Daisy grabbed Susan's arm. "No problem," she said to Eduardo. And to Fiona: "We'll wait out by the alley. Go talk."

When Fiona saw the tight expression on Eduardo's face, though, a sense of dread rose in her. "Can we talk" never meant anything good.

It was how her mother often started critical conversations. It was how her ex had informed her he'd be out of town for another business trip... Business trips that, she'd later learned, hadn't even existed but had served as cover for his life with his second family.

"I'm not happy about some things I heard this morning," Eduardo said. His voice wasn't kind and gentle like usual. It was sharp, almost angry.

It's happening again.

"My kids came home spouting misconceptions about our economic status and our Mexican heritage." He warmed to his topic. "Someone even gave your kids the notion that we're illegal immigrants, which is absolutely ridiculous. My kids and I are American citizens."

Somehow, her mother's words had gotten back to him. She opened her mouth to try to explain.

He didn't give her the chance. "I can't have that, Fiona. I want my kids to be proud of who they are and comfortable with the life I'm able to provide. What I heard this morning put that at risk."

What was the use of trying to discuss it? It had never done any good in the past. Arguing with her mom, pleading with her ex...all of it was basically useless.

"I don't… I didn't mean to… I mean, I'm sorry…" Her words tangled and she gave up, her shoulders slumping.

"Do you actually agree with the things my kids heard?" His voice was angry, accusatory. As if he'd already made up his mind, judged her and found her wanting.

She looked down to hide her distress. How could she argue back intelligently and convince him he was wrong about her especially when her heart was shattering into a thousand pieces? When the bright new hope she'd been nurturing was fading to black?

"Fiona, I thought we had something here. I was really starting to care for you." Anger and confusion clouded his eyes.

She had to speak up, to explain. But the words were stuck in her throat. She felt the same way as when she'd taken hard tests at school. The pressure was on, and she knew she was going to fail. Her heart pounded. It was hard to catch her breath.

She should have known it wasn't going to work with Eduardo. He was a wonderful, caring, appealing man.

And women like Fiona didn't get to have wonderful, caring, appealing men.

Words continued to fail her.

"I'd never have guessed you were on board

with what was said." His chin lifted and his shoulders squared. "My kids and I will be moving out."

The sudden declaration made her gasp. Images of their time together—working in the garden, helping their kids learn to be responsible dog owners, sharing a tender kiss—flashed through her mind in a steadily darkening kaleidoscope. She looked down so he wouldn't see the tears gathering in her eyes, nodded because she couldn't speak. And even if she could finally find the words, what would be the point now?

She turned and forced herself to walk toward Susan and Daisy rather than collapsing into a sobbing heap on the ground.

Up ahead, her friends stood at the gate that separated the carriage house's yard area from the alley. "You ready?" Susan asked, glancing up from her phone.

Daisy was waving at a couple of kids who were carrying fishing poles toward the creek.

Good, they weren't paying attention to her. Because no way could she talk about what had just happened without breaking down.

"Let's go!" Daisy said.

Fiona nodded and followed them blindly to their usual walking route.

Susan was pecking her fingers rapidly at her phone and nearly bumped into a parked car.

Daisy caught her elbow on one side and Fiona automatically took the other.

"Thanks," Susan said, still without looking up. "I said, 'Taking your mom for a walk. Your grandma's in the house, but you're in charge. K?' She'll be thrilled."

Fiona's mother-brain kicked in and she swallowed her tears. "But I didn't even talk to her…"

Susan's phone buzzed again, and Susan looked, smiled and held it out for Daisy and Fiona to see.

"KK?" Daisy asked. "How'd she learn texting shortcuts when this is her first day with a new phone?"

"Don't question it, just come on."

They headed through the residential section of Rescue River. But the beauty of the blooming redbuds and dogwoods, the sound of a lawn mower and the smell of fresh-cut grass had no power to lift Fiona's spirits.

He was leaving. It was over.

"We want to hear about your date with Eduardo last night," Daisy said.

"The date we helped set up," Susan added. "Man, did we do well or what?" She fist-bumped Daisy. "Tell us every single detail."

How could she begin to tell her friends what had happened in the past twenty-four hours? How she'd reached the heights of hope and excitement—maybe even love—with Eduardo.

And how it had all come crashing down.

Her phone buzzed and automatically she pulled it out.

The text was from Lauren.

Mr. Delgado says they're moving out on Monday. <frowny face> Can we take care of Sparkles until they find a new house?

She hadn't known she could feel worse, but the heaviness of a thousand stones pressed down on her. She hadn't just imagined it. It was really happening.

Her steps slowed, then stopped.

"What?" Daisy asked.

"What's wrong?" Susan put her hand on Fiona's arm.

She texted back.

Sure.

And then she looked from Susan to Daisy. "He's moving out of the carriage house. On Monday." Slowly, she started walking again.

"Why would he do that?" Daisy asked. "I thought they were staying through the end of the school year, at least."

"Maybe he found a house," Susan said. "Wasn't he looking to buy something?"

"They haven't found a place yet. He wants us to take care of his dog until they do." She felt like a robot, saying the words in a monotone. "It's because…because he's mad at me."

Amid her friends' questions and concerned glances, Fiona kept hearing her mother's voice: *Why would he choose you?*

She didn't know she'd said it aloud until Daisy and Susan tugged her to a halt. "He would choose you because you're wonderful," Daisy said.

"And beautiful and a good person and fun," Susan added.

Fiona shook her head. Her girlfriends would always staunchly defend her, but she knew her deficits.

"You have to talk to him," Susan said. "Confront him with it. Find out what's really going on."

"I already know what's going on," she said miserably. "I froze under pressure and didn't get a chance to explain before he walked away. Besides, he could have any woman in town. One with no baggage or a mom who would make him and his kids feel like less. He doesn't want anything more to do with me."

"Talk to him some more," Daisy urged.

Fiona shook her head. "I just don't think I can handle another rejection. Not this weekend. Not now."

Daisy and Susan glanced at each other. "I'm texting Dion," Daisy said.

"And I'm texting Sam."

"No, don't." But she didn't have the energy to stop them. To talk anymore. She just wanted to go home and crawl into bed.

But of course, that wasn't to be. When she got home, the place was in chaos. Kids crying, her mother ineffectually trying to force them to behave, the dog barking.

"Do you want us to…?" Daisy and Susan both asked in unison.

"No. I'll handle it." And she waved goodbye to them and waded in, feeling like a hundred-pound weight sat on her shoulders.

Mechanically, she hugged Poppy, who was crying. Got her a stuffed animal and some semi-healthy chips, and told Maya to sit with her and watch a princess movie. Maya was the only one who didn't seem upset—which was par for the course, and Fiona thanked God she had one non-sensitive child—but even she seemed to welcome a chance to relax and settle down.

"Mom," Fiona said wearily. "Get yourself a cup of coffee. I'm going to talk to Lauren and Ryan." And she led her two eldest out to the porch.

She didn't feel like talking, didn't want to confront this. But that was what you did as a single parent. You carried on even when you felt like you couldn't, because there was no one else to shoulder the load.

For a brief bright moment, she'd thought she and Eduardo might go forward together. But clearly, she'd been deluded. She was alone, and she'd better get used to it.

The cheerful blooms along her front sidewalk sent their fragrance to them on a warm breeze, and Fiona tried to take in their message. Rebirth. Redemption. Life springing forth from cold, frozen ground.

She was learning. Trying to, anyway.

Amid her sadness, a little righteous anger surfaced toward Eduardo. He'd pushed her away again, just as he'd done after they'd kissed.

By now, he should know her better. He should have given her a chance to explain. And, she acknowledged to herself, she should have used her newfound strength and self-understanding to insist on it.

When Lauren sniffled, Fiona's attention snapped back to the present moment. No matter what happened to her own dreams, her commitment to her kids' well-being was ironclad. "So what happened, exactly?" she asked Lauren.

"I hate this thing." Lauren pulled out her cell

phone and handed it to Fiona. "Tell Grandma I don't want it."

"You don't have to use it, but sure, we can give it back." Fiona pocketed the phone. "What's got you so upset?"

"Sofia's mad at me because she doesn't have one," she said. "And I was texting Tiffany and this girl named Raquel, and they wanted me to download these apps that you're not supposed to use until you're thirteen. I told them I wasn't allowed, and they called me a baby."

"You did the right thing," Fiona soothed her, a tiny sliver of light piercing the darkness in her heart. If Lauren could make a choice like that, against peer pressure, then Fiona had done something right as a mother, at least. She hugged Lauren. "I'm proud of you."

"Thanks, Mom. I want to make up with Sofia, but they're moving away."

"So I hear." Pain started to rise up in her again, but she stifled it down for her kids' sakes. She couldn't fall apart.

She looked at Brownie, who'd come outside with them. "So Brownie is going to have his mom visiting us for a little while, huh?"

"I don't know why they're moving. I wish they weren't," Lauren said.

Ryan cleared his throat. "I think I might know why. I hurt Diego's feelings."

"What happened?" She put an arm around her sensitive boy.

"We were talking about how his family didn't have as much money as ours. He was kind of jealous of my building set, and I told him he could play with it, even though Grammy said his kind of people weren't careful."

"You told him what Grammy said?"

Ryan nodded miserably. "And he got mad. And said he didn't want to play with it, anyway, or with me."

Poppy banged out through the screen door and squatted down to give her brother and sister hugs. "I told Mr. Delgado he didn't have to go back to Mex'co. Told him to marry Mommy and stay here."

"You did?" Lauren asked.

"You did?" Ryan's eyes widened.

"You did?" Fiona echoed, trying to wrap her mind around the umpteen ways this day had gone wrong. "Um…what did he say?"

"He didn't answer me," Poppy said.

Anger at her blunt, hurtful mother blazed in Fiona, but she tamped it down and beckoned to Maya, who'd been listening from inside the house. "All four of you, listen to me. What Grammy said was wrong. People come from all different places. Some have lots of money and some don't have very much, but God values us all the same, do you hear me? We're all the same in God's eyes. And He wants all of us to get along. We don't treat people differently based on where they're from, or what they look like, or how much money they have."

All four kids looked at her, eyes round, nodding. Of course, they knew all of that; she'd raised them that way, and where she'd fallen short, Sunday school had filled in and expanded on that basic lesson.

Unfortunately, her mother hadn't gotten the memo.

"I want you to stay out here while I talk to Grandma," she said. She couldn't fix things with Eduardo, but she could make sure her kids didn't suffer any more damage. She *wasn't* a weak woman who'd fall apart because of a man. She'd stayed strong for her kids before, and she could do it again.

"Are you mad at us?" Ryan asked.

"No. I'm not mad at you." She hugged each of them quickly and then went inside.

In the kitchen, she yanked out a chair across from her mother, who was drinking coffee. "I have something to discuss with you."

"My goodness, you sound angry."

"I am," she said. "First of all, the comments about weight have to stop. To me, but most of all, to my daughters."

"What comments about weight?" Her mother's eyes opened wide.

"Comments like 'You're not cooking that, are you?' and 'It's never too early to watch your weight.'"

"I can understand why you've always been sensitive about your weight," her mother said. "You're so tall, and when you put on the pounds…"

"That. Comments like that. I want you to say nothing at all about size or weight. To me or to the girls. Or to Ryan, for that matter."

"Nothing? That's a little extreme."

"Nothing. But even more important, I don't want to hear any more remarks about a person's ethnicity or financial status."

"I don't talk about those things!" her mother said indignantly. "And I don't appreciate you making me feel like some sort of bad person. What kind of a way is that to treat your mother?"

"My children repeated some of what you said this morning to the Delgado family."

"Oh, dear. Is that why they're leaving?" Her mother looked down, but the corners of her mouth turned up just a little.

Until this moment, Fiona had never thought her mother's negative comments had ill intent. She'd thought her remarks—the weight ones, at least—were a misguided way of trying to help. But her smirk now made it seem like she'd been *hoping* the kids would repeat her stereotypes to the Delgados.

"You're my mother," she said evenly. "And you're my children's grandmother, and I know you love us. I hope you'll stay for the rest of the weekend. But if you make one more remark that suggests that stereotyping and racism are okay, you're going to need to leave."

"Are you threatening your own mother?"

Fiona cocked her head to one side and studied the woman who'd raised her. She'd done so much for Fiona...and so much *to* Fiona as well. "I'm setting the conditions for you to be in my home, Mom," she said, gentling her voice. "I can't have toxicity here, harming me and my children. But if you're willing to take the high road in your conversations with us, you are welcome to stay." She blinked away the sudden tears that rose to her eyes. "I love you, Mom. I hope we can have a better relationship."

"I just care about you! I've worked so hard to be slim all my life and you just don't even... Do you *know* how long it's been since I ate macaroni and cheese?"

Fiona swallowed the lump in her throat and shook her head.

"And if you cared about yourself, you wouldn't go out with a Mexican!"

Anger heated Fiona's face and made her breath come fast. "Out."

"What?" Her mother's voice rose an octave.

Dry-eyed, Fiona found her phone and looked for the number of Ralph Montour, a man in town who ran a car service. "Go get your things together," she said to her mother while the phone was ringing.

"But…it's Easter weekend."

That gave Fiona a pang.

"Hello?" Ralph said.

"Would you be able to drive my mother to the airport?" she asked.

"Sure thing. Today?"

"Yes. Today."

"My flight's not until Monday!" her mother protested.

"I'll call the airport and pay to get it changed." She gave Ralph the address. "She'll be ready in an hour."

"Fiona!" Her mother's voice rose into hysteria and tears came into her eyes. "You can't do this to me! You're all I have!"

Fiona drew in a breath. "I can't have poison in my kids' lives."

"I'm sorry!" Her mother grabbed her hand. "Please. Don't send me away."

Looking at her mother's hand—perfectly manicured, yes, and sporting several expensive rings, but still wrinkled and age-spotted—Fiona's resolve faltered. Slowly, she pulled out a chair and sat back down, facing her mother, knee to knee. "Do you understand what it is I don't want you to say? Or imply? To me, or the kids, or anyone else in Rescue River?"

Her mother's chin shook and big tears stood in her eyes. "I understand."

"Do you? Do you really understand that it's what's in a person's heart that matters, rather than a dress size or a bank account?"

She nodded. "I... I suppose so. It's just not..." She trailed off, then met Fiona's eyes. "It's not how I was raised, and it's not how I've thought about things. Looks are important. Money is important."

Fiona shook her head. "No, Mom. They're not. And putting priority on those things will only lead to misery."

Her mother stared at the ground, her throat working.

"And there's more."

Her mother took a tissue and wiped her eyes. "What more do you want from me?"

"I want a promise that you won't comment about people from other ethnic backgrounds or races. Not to them, not to me and especially not to, or in front of, the kids." She leaned forward to emphasize her point. "God made the world with all types of people in it, and our job is to love each other, not put each other down."

Her mother nodded. "I know," she said very quietly.

"I mean it, Mom. All kinds of people live in Rescue River. You're going to see different skin colors and hear different languages, see different styles of dress. It's not okay to disparage them. If you do, you'll have to leave."

"Fine." Her mother let out a windy sigh.

Fiona's indignation was fading. "I'll call Ralph back and let him know you don't need a ride. But I've got him on speed dial."

"I understand."

"Okay." She knelt and gave her mother an awkward hug. "I've got one text I need to send, and then we'll have some iced tea and help the kids decorate eggs."

She went into the bathroom—the only place where she knew she could get a moment's privacy—and sat down on the edge of the tub. She contemplated calling Eduardo, but she figured the damage had already been done. She couldn't handle more confrontation, anyway. A woman only had so much strength.

She let her head fall into her hands. She didn't know if she'd been right to nearly kick her mom out, to lecture her, or to let her stay. She didn't know if there was any repair work that could be done with Eduardo. "Lord," she prayed, "help me. Show me the right thing to do."

A moment later, she heard loud voices in the kitchen—not angry, thankfully, just loud—and knew her alone time had come to an end.

She had to make a choice. Either she could cave in, be the weak woman she'd been in her marriage, or she could draw on the strength she'd gained from her community, her friends and her God.

She drew in a breath and typed a carefully worded text to Eduardo. Read it over and hit Send.

It probably wasn't going to fix anything. Eduardo was still a man, and though she was starting to realize how different he was from her husband, she knew he still had a lot of pride.

She liked that about him. He was proud of his heritage, proud of his work. Proud to be a strong man.

He was a strong father, too, and his decision to move out made sense. He had to protect his children and do what was best for them. They shouldn't have been subjected to the words they'd heard today.

What she'd texted him was unlikely to change that. But at least she'd tried.

Chapter Fourteen

Eduardo was throwing toys and games into a big box when there was a knock at the door of the carriage house.

For a moment his heart leaped. Was it Fiona?

But no. He couldn't hope for that. Because whatever she said, he couldn't allow it to convince him to stay, to go back to her. Their differences were too great, the potential damage to his kids too real.

"Eduardo?" It was Dion's deep voice. "Need to talk to you, my man."

Eduardo shoved back the box, wiped his face on his sleeve and went to the door. "Come in. Kind of busy, though."

Dion walked into the center of the living room, looked around at the boxes and the chaos, and whistled. "You're serious about moving."

He nodded. "Mind if I keep packing while we talk? You can grab a soda from the fridge."

Dion slapped his back, hard. "I'll get both of us sodas. You can take a fifteen-minute break and listen to what I have to say, can't you?"

Eduardo didn't want to. He didn't want to lose momentum. He would rather not talk to anyone; just keep moving so he didn't have to think.

But he respected the older man, so he nodded. "Sure. I'll get the drinks."

"Sit on the porch?"

Eduardo shook his head. "Better to stay inside."

"Where are the kids?"

"They're with Lou Ann Miller. I... I didn't want them to see all this. They're upset enough. But they'll be back soon, so..."

"So hurry up and speak my piece? All right." Dion kept looking out the window, though. And a moment later, Eduardo saw why when Sam Hinton knocked on the door.

Eduardo narrowed his eyes at Dion. "Was this planned?" he asked as he went to let Sam in.

"Get the man a beverage."

Sighing, Eduardo did so. His friends were good men, no denying it, but they'd try to talk him out of what he was doing. And he couldn't let them succeed.

He walked back into the living room, shoved

the soda can at Sam and sat down. "You guys have fifteen minutes. I'm watching the clock."

"What's prompting the move out?" Sam asked.

"I need a better environment for my kids."

"Seems like they've been happy here, from what Susan has told me."

"They were. Until Fiona's mother arrived to rub in all our differences. Economic and...background."

Dion frowned. "What did she say? Anything you haven't heard before?"

"It's not about me," Eduardo said. "I understand that some people didn't grow up knowing how to deal with differences. But she said stuff that Fiona's kids picked up and repeated to mine."

"Stuff about your being Latino?" Sam asked.

Eduardo nodded. "And poor."

Dion lifted an eyebrow. "Are you poor, or just a tightwad? Nobody I know saves as much as you do."

Eduardo glared. "It's called *frugal*. I spend money on what's important."

"Nothing for anyone to criticize there," Sam said. "Besides, the way your business is taking off, you're headed toward being extremely comfortable, financially."

Eduardo waved a hand. "That's all beside the

point. The big problem is that Fiona agrees with her mother."

"She *does*?" Sam frowned. "Where'd you get that idea?"

"I told her about what happened, and she didn't even get upset. She just walked away. She didn't care."

"Let me ask you something," Sam said. "Does the Fiona you know seem like a person who'd agree with that nonsense? Who wouldn't care that children had been hurt and stereotypes perpetuated?"

He looked at his hands and instantly knew the answer. Slowly, he shook his head. "That's not how she is."

"What I'm wondering," Dion said, "is whether you're going to let one ignorant woman push you out of your home."

"And away from the woman you love," Sam added.

"Hey, hey now!" Eduardo tried to wave away the words. "Nobody said anything about love."

"But it's the truth, isn't it?" Dion asked quietly. The question hung in the air.

"I do love her," Eduardo said slowly. "But I have to protect my kids."

"From what, ignorance?" Dion shook his head. "They're going to face that in this world. It's not okay, and I hope one day it will change, but right now that's the society we live in. Their names and their coloring, everyone's going to know they're Mexican, even though they've grown up here in the Midwest. Better teach them how to deal with it rather than running away."

Eduardo had opened his mouth to speak, but now he closed it. Was that what he was doing? Running away?

Was that what he wanted to model to his kids?

He knew it wasn't. Sam and Dion were right.

Were they right about the rest of it, too? Could he stay and try to make a go of things with Fiona, as they seemed to be suggesting?

He rubbed the back of his neck and didn't look at them. "How am I supposed to manage the fact that Fiona has so much more money than I do? Her kids have stuff I wouldn't buy my kids in a million years."

Sam frowned. "I don't think of Fiona as being real materialistic, nor teaching her kids to be that way."

"I've seen her shopping at the discount store, like everyone else," Dion added. "What do her kids have that your kids want?"

"Cell phone, the latest Lego kit…" Eduardo trailed off. When he said it aloud, it didn't sound like a big deal.

"She got her kids cell phones?" Sam asked.

"I think her mom brought along a bunch of

expensive gifts." Which wasn't Fiona's fault, of course, any more than the sacks of candy his own parents gave to his kids could be blamed on him.

Dion leaned back in his chair, cradling his head in his interlaced hands. "I get where you're coming from with the money thing, for sure. I mean…" He glanced at Sam. "I have feelings for a Hinton. Daisy could buy me and everything I own with her pocket change."

Sam narrowed his eyes at Dion. "Money doesn't matter, but you're an old man compared to her."

"She doesn't seem to mind," Eduardo said mildly. He understood that Sam was protective of his sister, but you couldn't miss the way Dion and Daisy looked at each other.

"We're not talking about me." Dion deliberately turned away from Sam to focus on Eduardo. "We're talking about you, and how you're making some stiff-necked move that has your kids *and* Fiona's kids *and* Fiona herself crying their eyes out."

"Fiona's been crying?"

"So I hear."

"She's a good woman," Sam said. "Pretty good friends with me and Susan these last few years, and I haven't seen a mean bone in her body. Good mother, good Christian, humble…"

"A looker," Dion contributed.

"Hey!" Eduardo glared at him.

"She *is* pretty," Sam said.

"And if you don't like us noticing," Dion said, "how're you gonna like it when some other guy steps in and claims her because you had too much pride to court a rich woman?"

"What do your kids think of her?" Sam asked.

"They love her. Sofia was hesitant, at first, because of loyalty to her mom. But she and Fiona seem to be getting close."

"And would they love a woman who looked down on them for their background?"

Eduardo didn't answer, but he knew they wouldn't. His kids had good instincts about people. They knew Fiona's heart was in the right place.

They all sat there a couple of minutes, watching the soundless baseball game on the television.

"You sure you're not feeling some survivor's guilt?" Sam asked abruptly. "When your wife dies, it can be hard to let her go and move on to being happy with another woman. Believe me, I struggled with that."

Eduardo shrugged a little. "Could be." Elizabeth would have encouraged him to move on and find love again; they'd even talked about it. But until now, his sense that he hadn't been enough of a protector had kept him from doing that.

"Have you taken it to the Lord?" Dion asked.

"I…" Eduardo stopped. He'd prayed some, sure. And he'd expressed his anger to the Lord when his kids had been hurt that morning. But had he really prayed before deciding to move out?

Voices and clomping footsteps broke into their meeting, which, Eduardo realized now, had gone on quite a bit longer than fifteen minutes. "Dad, we're home," Diego called.

Both kids stopped when they saw the other two men there, altered their usual manner into company politeness and shook hands.

"Hey, you two," Dion said. "How'd you like to do a little fishing with Mr. Hinton and me?"

"And then have some burgers at my house?" Sam added.

Eduardo looked at his kids and then at his friends. "Let me talk to them for a minute," he said.

"Take your time," Sam said. "I'm heading home to start those burgers. They'll be good, and Mindy will be glad to have somebody to play with."

"I've got fishing poles in the back of my car," Dion said. "Come on out when you decide."

"Thanks." Eduardo clapped them both on the backs as they walked to the door.

On the porch table, he noticed the phone he hadn't looked at in hours. Reflexively, he picked it up and checked.

One text.

From Fiona.

He clicked on it.

Whatever you may think of me, I don't want your kids to feel like they've been kicked out or that I feel the same way my mother does. I'm sorry for the things my kids said to yours. It won't happen again.

And then he turned back to find both of his kids looking at him with puppy-dog eyes.

"Do we *have* to move, Dad?" Sofia asked. "I'm sorry I talked about wanting a phone. I don't want one anymore and, anyway, I think Lauren's mom is taking hers away."

"And Diego said I could play with his Lego set. I don't need one of my own."

"And we don't care if we're poor," Sofia said.

"We're not…" Eduardo scrubbed a hand over his face. "We have plenty. More than a lot of people in the world. And material things aren't what's important, anyway."

"We know that!" Sofia said.

"So can we stay here, Dad, please?" Diego begged.

Eduardo looked over his shoulder through the screen door. There was Fiona's house. Probably, there was Fiona.

And her kids. And her mother.

He went to the door. "Hey, Dion," he called after his friend. "Instead of taking my kids fishing, how would you feel about babysitting six kids a little later? I've got something to set up."

"Six kids and two dogs," Diego added. "Don't forget Sparkles and Brownie."

Dion spun and strode back toward him, a wide grin on his face. "Sounds like I might need some help, but I'm completely game for it. I'll see if Daisy can come over."

"Do that," Eduardo said. "Because I've got some work to do."

"You want to *what*?" Fiona said to her mother after they'd eaten a late dinner.

"I want to take care of the children while you mend fences with Eduardo," she said. "He's actually quite charming."

Fiona blinked. "When did you talk to Eduardo?"

"When you were fixing dinner."

"Oka-a-a-ay," Fiona said. "But…are you sure

Eduardo wants to talk to me? And are you sure you can manage the kids?"

"I have help," her mother said, pointing out the window.

Dion and Daisy stood halfway between the carriage house and the big house, talking heatedly. Then they smiled. Then laughed. And then Dion opened his arms to give Daisy a long hug.

Fiona looked over at her mother. "You're sure about this?"

Her mother squared her shoulders. "I'm sure. Go on now. He's waiting for you."

So, Fiona walked down her front walk and there was Eduardo. Not in his truck, but on foot. He was so handsome he took her breath away. "Take a walk?" he asked.

He must want to apologize, maybe explain his moving out. It wasn't much, but it was all she was going to get, and she wasn't going to waste it. She was going to treasure every remaining moment with this man.

"Okay, sure." They fell into step together, walking down to the back of her property, to a path that wound between the cornfields and the old barn.

Before she could lose her nerve, she spoke up. "I'm sorry about my mom," she said. "Between her gifts and the things she said…translated through the brains of little kids… I'm not surprised you'd be offended. That you'd want to move out."

"I'm sorry I blamed you for your mom."

"If it helps, she's going to try not to do it again. I gave her an ultimatum."

He lifted an eyebrow. "Ever done that before?"

"No. But I should have."

They walked along together, the creek beside them rippling.

"I… I think I was premature in saying I wanted to move out," he said finally.

"Really?" Hope sprung up inside her.

"The kids are really upset."

It was all about the kids, then. And that was fine. Good, even. "Mine were, too."

"And I was upset, too, Fiona, because the truth is…" He stopped and took her two hands in his so he was facing her. "The truth is I don't want to move out. I want to…" He looked up at the darkening sky.

All of a sudden, she felt like she was going to explode. "Look, Eduardo, I'm sorry about what happened, and I hope you'll stay for the kids' sakes. But I can't deal with this semi-romantic vibe we've got going here. It's making me crazy. Kissing me, letting me get close, then pulling back… I don't want to be treated that way."

Instead of answering, he tugged her to the edge of the cornfield. "Look at that."

"Aww, fireflies." Her heart softened.

"No, over here."

"Aaaah!" Fiona jumped closer to Eduardo when she saw what looked like two giant people.

He put an arm around her. "They're not going to hurt you. Come meet them."

A couple of steps later, Fiona realized how foolish she'd been for being afraid as she looked up at the cheerful straw pair dressed in colorful rags.

"They're *scarecrows*! But…they weren't here before, were they?"

"They're new." He paused, then added, "Take a look at her necklace."

Fiona moved forward and bent toward the female scarecrow. Something sparkled around her straw neck.

Her heart gave a great thump. She glanced back at Eduardo.

He was watching her, a nervous smile on his face. When she smiled back, he stepped behind the scarecrow, unfastened the beautiful necklace and came back to hold it out, showing her.

"Do you like it? It's been in my family for over a hundred years, but I know a lot of women like more modern styles. Elizabeth did. I just… Well, I treasure this necklace, and I'd like for you to wear it if you like it, too."

"I love it," she said honestly. "But I don't really *get* it."

He grasped her hand in both of his. "Can you forgive me for being so hot and cold? For having baggage and taking a while to figure things out?"

She hesitated.

"That's why I made the scarecrows. Because I've been scared. Scared of not being a good enough protector and provider. Of just not being, well, *enough*."

His heartfelt confession and the sincerity in his eyes tugged at her heart. "Of course you're good enough. You're wonderful." She stole a glance at the necklace, an intricately wrought silver pendant crowned by a large round diamond. A family heirloom. So much what she would have chosen herself.

"Fiona, I know we need to get to know each other better. I know it's too soon to make a commitment. But I'd like to work toward that with you. I want you to have this as a symbol of the future we might have together, with God's help."

She stared into those liquid brown eyes and tried to breathe.

"Because I love you, Fiona. I love your gentleness and your energy and the love you give your children. And maybe this is shallow, but I love how gorgeous you are."

The tone of his voice was sincere and so was his face. And in the warmth of that, the last hard, brittle fragments of her own not-good-enough worries melted away. She stepped closer to him. "I love you, too, Eduardo. And yes." She paused, her chest filled with amazement. "I would be incredibly honored to wear this and get to know you better and maybe…at least, think about building a life together. If our kids agree."

He clasped her to him then—a tight embrace that enveloped her, promising strength and safety and, most of all, love. Minutes later, he softened the embrace and pulled her to his side. "As for the kids," he said, "mine adore you. And I think—based on what she said this afternoon—that Poppy is going to be able to accept me. She was the toughest case."

"All of my kids will be thrilled." She leaned against him, still hardly able to believe it. Eduardo had said he loved her. He wanted to make a commitment to her.

He shifted so he could study her face. "How do you feel about our economic differences? I don't have as much money as you do."

She shrugged. "Doesn't matter to me. I didn't earn my money."

There was a great rustling and shushing in the bushes beside them. Brownie ran out into the clearing and started barking at the scarecrows. Sparkles limped over and nudged him as if in reassurance, and he quieted and went to sit at Fiona's side.

A moment passed and then all six kids burst out, some from the bushes and some from the cornfield. "Get married, get married, get married," they chanted.

Fiona pressed a hand to her mouth, whether to stop laughter or tears, she couldn't say.

"Come here, all of you," Eduardo said. "Sit down."

So the kids sat in a circle around them, with Brownie and Sparkles joining in, climbing from lap to lap.

"Were you kids listening to what we said?" Eduardo asked them, his voice serious.

Lauren and Sofia glanced at each other. "We weren't exactly *listening*," Lauren said.

"We just *overheard* a couple of things," Sofia added.

"Like that you might get committed," Diego nearly shouted.

"That means married!" Lauren and Sofia said together.

"Get married, get married," Ryan started, and the others took up the chorus again.

Fiona looked at her youngest, who was participating in the chant but looking a bit confused. "How do you feel, Poppy?" she asked. "What if we became a family, after we've thought about it more?"

"Would I still be the baby?" she asked.

Fiona glanced at Eduardo to find him looking at her. He leaned closer and whispered in her ear. "Do you think we might have just one more baby, together?"

Fiona closed her eyes against the sudden tears of joy that sprang up in them.

Eduardo got it. He loved babies and kids. He didn't see seven kids as excessive. If all this worked out, they'd have one more opportunity, if God blessed them with it, at having a baby again, at raising it together.

She reached out to tug Poppy onto her lap. "You'll always be my very special Poppy."

"And I think you're special, too," Eduardo added. "Every one of you kids. You're God's gift to us."

"And if we were blessed with one more gift, what could be more perfect?" Fiona murmured to him beneath the children's excited chatter. "I'd love to have one more. With you."

Epilogue

One Year Later

Fiona knelt to adjust the maroon-and-ivory ribbons on the sides of the seats and checked the aisle's white runner for folds and rough spots.

"Mom, what are you doing?" Lauren scolded. "It's almost time for the wedding to start!"

"I just want everything to be perfect," she said.

Eduardo appeared and held out his hands, tugging her to her feet. "Everything is perfect. Come relax for half an hour before the ceremony."

"I need to—"

"You need to relax," he said firmly and guided her toward a corner of the newly renovated Farmingham Wedding Barn. "Sit," he said, holding a chair for her and then pulling up another beside her. "Are you feeling okay?"

"I'm fine, Eduardo!" But she let her hands rest over the bump of her belly, propped her feet on a hay bale and admitted to herself that it felt good to sit down.

Eduardo was the most caring of husbands, especially now that she was in her seventh month of pregnancy. It had all happened fast, but it was what had worked, what they'd wanted. They were madly in love and couldn't wait to be husband and wife, and anyway, with six kids, there wasn't time or space for a long, drawn-out courtship. Although, she and Eduardo *had* taken a lovely honeymoon to a small island off the coast of Florida.

Fortunately, all the kids were thrilled about the new little brother to come.

"Go away! You're not supposed to see me!" Miss Minnie's shrill, nervous voice cut through the barn's peaceful quiet. Her niece and several other friends spoke to her in soothing tones, straightening her simple ivory gown.

And then Mr. Love, resplendent in a grey tuxedo and red vest, approached his bride on his granddaughter's arm. "I know the groom isn't supposed to see the bride before the ceremony," he said, "but that's not a problem for me." He touched the sunglasses that shaded his unseeing eyes. "Can't look at much of anything, but I can imagine plenty. I know you're a gorgeous sight to behold."

Fiona turned to Eduardo as the elders made their way to the back of the barn. "I'm just thrilled that they're the first couple to marry in this barn."

"They won't be the last." A deep voice behind her startled her, and she turned to see Daisy and Dion.

Daisy thrust her left hand in front of Fiona's face. "He just proposed!" she practically screamed.

"That's wonderful!" Fiona hugged her friend, who looked like she now had all the happiness in the world, while Eduardo pumped Dion's hand.

The children were leading guests to their seats and the minister gave them a wave, and she nodded. They were ready.

Mr. Love and Miss Minnie, ready to start anew in their eighties.

Daisy and Dion, finally overcoming their barriers and committing to a life of love together.

And she and Eduardo... She'd no sooner had the thought when he wrapped his arms around her from behind. "I love you so much."

"I love you, too."

As the guitar and piano music began and Poppy scattered rose petals along the short aisle between the rows of chairs, Fiona closed her eyes.

Her business. Her friends. Her children. All thriving.

And the love between herself and Eduardo… blossoming and growing. And coming to fruition in the child that grew inside her.

"Thank you, Father," she whispered as the congregation stood and the "Wedding March" began.

* * * * *

If you enjoyed this story, try these other books in the RESCUE RIVER *miniseries from Lee Tobin McClain!*

ENGAGED TO THE SINGLE MOM
HIS SECRET CHILD
SMALL-TOWN NANNY
THE SOLDIER AND THE SINGLE MOM
THE SOLDIER'S SECRET CHILD

Available now from Love Inspired!

Find more great reads at
www.LoveInspired.com

Dear Reader,

Have you ever struggled with body image? I think most of us do at one time or another. I was a beanpole kid and teenager. It doesn't seem fair that I morphed into "carrying a few extra pounds" without even a pause at the perfect weight.

Or wait…maybe that's because perfection is an unattainable goal?

In *A Family for Easter*, Fiona struggles with her size, and her challenge is exacerbated by her mother's criticism. Because she feels so imperfect, she isn't open to receiving the love Eduardo offers. It takes caring friends and the realization that she's passing her own body-image issues down to her daughter to make her see that she's "fearfully and wonderfully made," God's perfect creation.

As you put on your Easter finery this year, my prayer is that you see yourself as God's good creation, ready to focus on His joyous resurrection.

Happy Easter!
Lee

Get 2 Free Books,

Plus 2 Free Gifts—

just for trying the Reader Service!

Love Inspired. **SUSPENSE**

Get 2 Free Books,
Plus 2 Free Gifts—
just for trying the Reader Service!

HOME on the RANCH

YES! Please send me the **Home on the Ranch Collection** in Larger Print. This collection begins with 3 FREE books and 2 FREE gifts in the first shipment. Along with my 3 free books, I'll also get the next 4 books from the Home on the Ranch Collection, in LARGER PRINT, which I may either return and owe nothing, or keep for the low price of $5.24 U.S./ $5.89 CDN each plus $2.99 for shipping and handling per shipment*. If I decide to continue, about once a month for 8 months I will get 6 or 7 more books, but will only need to pay for 4. That means 2 or 3 books in every shipment will be FREE! If I decide to keep the entire collection, I'll have paid for only 32 books because 19 books are FREE! I understand that accepting the 3 free books and gifts places me under no obligation to buy anything. I can always return a shipment and cancel at any time. My free books and gifts are mine to keep no matter what I decide.

268 HCN 3760 468 HCN 3760

Name	(PLEASE PRINT)	
Address		Apt. #
City	State/Prov.	Zip/Postal Code

Signature (if under 18, a parent or guardian must sign)

Mail to the **Reader Service**:
IN U.S.A.: P.O. Box 1867, Buffalo, NY. 14240-1867
IN CANADA: P.O. Box 609, Fort Erie, Ontario L2A 5X3

HRCBPA18

READERSERVICE.COM

Manage your account online!

- Review your order history
- Manage your payments
- Update your address

> *We've designed the*
> *Reader Service website*
> *just for you.*

Enjoy all the features!

- Discover new series available to you, and read excerpts from any series.
- Respond to mailings and special monthly offers.
- Browse the Bonus Bucks catalog and online-only exculsives.
- Share your feedback.

Visit us at:
ReaderService.com